BEYOND THE BEACH HUTS

Beyond the Beach Huts

Writers of Whitstable

ISBN 978-0-9935492-0-5

Writers of Whitstable are proud to support Trust Sulha, a small locally based charity supporting the education of Afghan refugee children and young people in Pakistan since 2002.

We are grateful to Canterbury City Council for their support.

Published in the UK in 2016 by Coinlea Publishing
www.coinlea.co.uk
Printed and bound in Great Britain by Clays Ltd, St Ives plc
Typesetting: Coinlea Services
Cover design: David Williamson
Editing team: Lin White, Joanne Bartley, John Wilkins

Contents

Foreword

'Have you ever tasted a Whitstable oyster?'

These are the first words of *Tipping the Velvet*, a bracing coming of age story of a Victorian oyster girl, written by a former Whitstable resident, Sarah Waters.

Waters is not the only writer to be inspired by the town or its famous 'natives', for here, *Beyond the Beach Huts* offers every kind of Whitstable tale.

There are gulls, pebbles, sunsets, the sea – but look deeper. There's more to Whitstable than oysters. Much, much more.

Take a walking tour through Whitstable's twisty lanes and irreverent history, with tips on how to catch a sighting of the DFL and the even rarer Crabzilla. See the town with fresh eyes on a surprising treasure hunt with Joanne Bartley, the founder of Writers of Whitstable.

There are tales of arrival, of finding your feet in a brand new place. In Alison Kenward's story a woman makes an unlikely new friend, while Nick Hayes' tale, set on Tankerton Slopes, shows the moment of change that makes great leaps possible.

There are tales of leaving, of reconciling with the past, as in Laura Sehjal's poignant *The Pink Glove*, and with a possible future, in AJ Ivory's moving piece.

As the tide ebbs and flows, Whitstable is always changing, though it is tied to the sea. Off the coast of Whitstable, fishermen in Kim Miller's tale make an unexpected catch. In Lin White's tale, the wrench of emigration, while James

Dutch's *The Olive Branch* tells the pain of change, unwanted.

In our seaside town known for traffic jams that can be caused by one parked car in a loading bay, the town is brought to a standstill in David Williamson's story while in *Whitstable Parking is On the Agenda*, a new councillor has an ingenious solution. Beyond the High Street, there are spots any local will know – The Street, Cushing's Seat, Squeeze Gut Alley, the Neptune. There are old traditions, from the building of grotters with Nick Hayes and my *Oyster Wife*, and new, the fickle art scene in *The Private View* and the lure of pubs, in John Wilkins' tale set in the Duke, and among the oyster beds.

And as this is an old town, an ancient settlement, there is every kind of haunting with deliciously creepy tales by Phillip Mind and RJ Dearden.

Spooky, funny, tense, atomic, dark with magic, despair and hope. If you're ready for a taste of Whitstable in story form, turn the page. We have just the thing…

Peggy Riley

Author of Amity & Sorrow and Whitstable writer

Peggy Riley is an author and playwright, living in Whitstable. Her first novel, *Amity & Sorrow*, was published in the US, UK & Commonwealth, and translated for publication in France, Italy, and the Netherlands. Her short fiction has won prizes with Bridport, MsLexia and was shortlisted for the 2016 Costa Short Story Award. When she first moved to Whitstable, she ran a literature development project for the region, East Kent Live Lit, encouraging good new writing in unusual spaces and contexts. She regularly runs workshops in schools, arts centres, universities and prisons.

The Ruff Plannit Guide
to Whitstable

by Hermarnie Jesuiter

WHITSTABLE (*Pron: Whit-sta-bul*) lies 51 miles due East of London and is a worthy stopping-off point for visitors wishing to explore the north coast of KENT. Much of what we see today was formed initially during the Triassic, Cretaceous and more recently in the Tertiary period of earth's history. This small coastal town has a rich history waiting to be discovered. Indeed, a full morning or an afternoon could easily be devoted to exploring its many attractions, curiosities and the bohemian atmosphere that has developed in more recent decades.

HISTORY

Visiting the town in 1785, **Samuel Johnson** wrote 'When a man tires of Whitstable he tires of life; for there is in Whitstable all that life can afford, at a modest price.' **Charles Dickens** was less complimentary when he visited the town in 1871, bestowing a mere seven words when recalling his visit: 'They eat a lot of oysters here.' The Romans were the first recorded settlers to the town, attracted by the abundance of the native oyster. In AD 43, **Emperor Claudius**, during his first invasion of Southern Britain, instructed his Commander-in-Chief, **Aulus Plautius**, to allocate small glass phials of wine vinegar to each soldier of the Legion 'So that they might better enjoy and digest this abundant harvest.' The **Tabasco Stone**, situated in a field accessed by path from the road in nearby SWALE-CLIFFE, and well worth the short walk from the centre of the town, is a rare relic of the period. Inscriptions carved deeply into the stone reveal that many in the Legion were dissatisfied with their meagre ration of vinegar, protesting that their requests for bottles of Tabasco sauce had been continually ignored by the senile old Emperor.

The observant visitor will not fail to miss the brightly painted inscription on the reverse of the stone 'Gaz 'n' Mandy 4 eva.' Academic historians from the nearby **University of Kent** fail to agree on the meaning of this, but the general consensus is that this is most likely a later addition.

The Vikings visited the town briefly in May AD 814. Local inhabitants hostile to the threat of immigrants gave resistance. **Kirk Son of Douglas** and **Antowulf Kurtis**, leaders of the Viking fleet, ordered their men to camp at nearby TANKERTON, much like today, a more affluent and pleasant neighbourhood and more accepting of their Norse visitors. After a few days of slaughter and pillage, and in fear that the mud hut property price index might plummet, they too took arms against the Viking invaders and the fleet were forced to retreat to HERNE BAY where they were eaten alive by the local community, much as the modern-day visitor to the town might be greeted.

Centuries passed, and Whitstable remained a minor settlement until the rise of the Industrial Revolution. Population growth in the major cities saw the demand rise for fish and the economy of the town flourished well into the middle of the 20th Century. The two town quays, the accurately named EAST QUAY and WEST QUAY, are still the hub of fishing activity and offer the visitor an authentic fishing port still at work, although at time of writing plans are currently in place by local councillors to develop the WEST QUAY into a mixed cultural and leisure attraction. This has allegedly both angered many local residents and allegedly 'surprised' property developers who were hoping the proposed regeneration scheme, potentially attracting new branches of **Starbucks** and **Subway**, would destroy the character of the quays irreversibly. The harder to find EAST QUAY, hidden from view by the picturesque and other-worldly **Aggregates Factory**, will for now remain unspoilt and remote.

FAMILIARISING YOURSELF

To fully enjoy the Whitstable experience, an appreciation of local idiosyncrasies is advised. The dialect can often confuse foreign tourists and visitors arriving from other parts of the UK. A girl should be referred as a gel, a man a geezer, and as in many places in the South of England, you are best advised to refer to minors as kids. Deploying the word children will only confuse the person you are speaking with.

The phenomenon of the **DFL** (Down from London) in recent years has been a mixed blessing for the town. The eagerness of DFLs to buy property in the town has been a Godsend to local Estate Agents. Lines of top-of-the-range BMWs and Audis parked at the back of their offices demonstrate the enormous gratitude they owe to their DFL clients. If the town captivates you, and if your Canary Wharf salary allows, you can pick up a property that is comparable to what you might pay in Monaco, without all the inconvenient hassle of travelling to the Côte d'Azur. For a modest £500,000 (at current prices) you can easily acquire a cottage-style two-bedroom terrace house. Of course this will come without a garden or private parking or central heating and will still require renovation, but with a little TLC and a new damp course, and maybe a new roof too, you will be at the heart of this charming town, only minutes away from the three and a half thousand coffee shops on your doorstep.

If you want something more modest, then a **beach hut** by the sea is a snip at around £50,000, and a great location in which to observe all the murders that allegedly take place close by.

Whilst making hard-working Estate Agents as rich as

Croesus, the arrival of the DFL has also altered the social fabric of the town. The DFL has given rise to local people adopting a new mantra 'A new me, a new life.' Being priced out of the local property market by the DFLs seeking second, or indeed third homes by the sea, many are seeing this as a 'golden opportunity' to re-locate to Margate or Gravesend in search of a new beginning.

As you wander around the town you will be delighted by the many curious names the town has given to its streets and alley ways. **Squeeze Gut Alley** and **Joy Lane** are but a few. Some facts the town can lay claim to include the local myth of an over-sized crab terrorising the local waters. **Crabzilla** has been sighted on several occasions by local seamen and townsfolk, although descriptions to its actual size and dimensions often have a direct correlation to the amount of alcohol consumed by those who report seeing it. The local phenomenon of **The Street**, a shingle spit stretching out into the sea, is not to be missed, and at low tide visitors can walk out for nearly a quarter of a mile offshore. This was a popular pursuit for many years until the arrival of Crabzilla and fears of crustacean abduction.

Another point of interest if you are by the beach is that the **Island Wall** is not a wall, neither is it an island, but an indeterminate stretch of houses and former fishing huts running parallel to the sea; many property developers are allegedly excited that careful mismanagement by local planning officers may allegedly afford them a loophole to build expensive apartments for DFLs within the Island Wall vicinity, and there may even be the prospect of enticing new cultural attractions such as **Starbucks** and **Subway** into the area in the years ahead, creating at least five desperately needed new part-time jobs in the town.

Perhaps the most famous son of Whitstable is **Peter Cushing**, the mild-mannered actor best known for his roles in Hammer House horror genre films of the 1950s and 1960s. The town has other residents and famous visitors too, including **Harry**

Hill (Comedian), famous for his large-collared shirts and spectacles, **Suggs** (Vocalist) of hilarious nutty 80s boy band Madness, **Janet Street-Porter** (Famous for) and for several hours a few years ago the pop genius, **Kid Creole**.

CULTURAL ATTRACTIONS

For a town located so close to the sea, Whitstable is unusual in having no main promenade, no central park, pier or bandstand, but what it lacks in tourist infrastructure is compensated by the array of cultural attractions. No visit to the town would be complete without a walk down the length of the **High Street** from the WEST QUAY to the RAILWAY BRIDGE.

If you see a throng of visitors a few doors down at the entrance to **Ron's Plaice**, do not be surprised. This famous fish and chip shop is a magnet for fans of the Hollywood blockbuster series *Star Wars*. Film buffs will instantly recognise the interior of the café as one of the settings from *The Empire Strikes Back* where Luke Skywalker famously buys a bag of chips for R2D2 and C3PO. Ron allows photos to be taken with him next to the frying range for a modest charge and souvenir sachets of Star Wars ketchup and brown sauce can also be purchased for a modest charge.

Taking a U-turn, head back up the High Street passing an array of art galleries. Whitstable's art scene has flourished in recent decades. Where once only a few middle-aged blokes sporting beards, tweed waistcoats and wearing Converse plimsolls could be found painting pictures and welding bits of old junk together, now there are thousands. Good examples of contemporary local art work can be found at the **Print Block**, a hidden gem showcasing contemporary silk screen prints, and on the walls of **Ron's Plaice**, but the Mecca for most visitors is the Whitstable **Horsebridge Centre**. Exhibitions are frequent here and you will always find paintings and drawings of fishing boats in the West Quay harbour at modest prices, ideal souvenirs of the town to hang on the living room wall.

If contemporary post-modern urban art is your bag, then a visit to the cubicles in the **Public Lavatories** near the quays is essential. Here you will find depictions of both male and female anatomy executed in naïve and monochromatic gestural markings together with opinions about the vicissitudes of national football teams, where the visitor can easily while away half an hour or so checking for spelling mistakes.

Another interesting fact is that Whitstable boasts more pull-along shopping trolleys per head of population than anywhere else in the world, easily surpassing other trolley 'hot spots' such as Eastbourne and Bridlington.

Recognising this USP, inspired local councillors sought over many years to bid for European Regional Development Funding, and in 2004 at the peak of European money being squandered by Brussels the **Shopping Trolley Museum** opened, a short walk from the Island Wall. The Museum houses a fine collection of pull-along shopping trolleys most often associated with elderly ladies. Trolleys from across the centuries and from as far afield as Penzance can be found here. The bulk of the collection was amassed locally from the many hundreds of trolleys that are left abandoned outside shops and next to bus stops each year.

Royal Stewart and Black Watch tartans are by far the most common designs on display, but pride of place is reserved for the Museum's oldest and rarest artefact, the **Robert the Bruce's Trolley**. This fine example dating back to 1306 was in the personal possession of the Bruce himself and academic historians from the nearby University of Kent believe it to have been instrumental in the Bruce's defeat of Edward II and the English army at the Battle of Bannockburn in 1314.

Opened to great fanfare by pop legend **Kid Creole** (and his backing band the Coconuts) in 2005, local councillors were justly proud when their vision for economic regeneration was awarded the 'Runner Up' prize in the Annual Tourist Attraction of the Year Awards (Whitstable and Herne Bay District category) in the same year.

Take a sharp left and you find yourself on Whitstable's long stretch of shingle beach with fine views over the delightfully grey estuary. Taking care to avoid the many varieties of dog dirt on display here, there is nothing finer on a sunny day than to stroll along this stretch of coastline. Still well preserved on both the Island Wall beach and EAST QUAY beach are other landmarks long associated with the town, the hundreds of brightly painted **beach huts**. If you are a DFL looking to buy one, don't let the locals, who are invariably envious of your spending power, put you off with their dire warnings about the huts.

For reasons unknown, the beach huts have acquired something of a reputation for sinister goings-on. All manner of dark deeds are supposed to happen near the huts in the twilight hours, murders being by far the most common. This has fuelled a small industry of amateur writers specialising in the detective-murder genre to use the beach huts as a setting for many of their fictional dramas; this is in stark contrast to the actual number of murders recorded in the vicinity by the local constabulary. With only two reported murders from both the 19th and 20th centuries combined, the town boasts an enviable ratio of 1:3264 real to fictional murders committed, making it simultaneously one of the most common places in Britain to be killed, and the least likely.

Whitstable is at its busiest during the weeks of the **Oyster Festival** in early August. The town fills with visitors, and is one of the few times of the year when DFLs will stay in their properties here. The festival celebrates the princely oyster and thousands are consumed with many visitors trying the slimy, briny delicacy for the first time. This provides a great boost for local pharmacists when the demand for Imodium capsules and bottles of Pepto-Bismol reaches its peak.

SHOPPING, FOOD AND ACCOMMODATION

The shopaholics among you won't be disappointed by the array of tempting goods for sale. As you stroll along the High Street you will still find speciality shops reminiscent of times past and of the type now all but disappeared from so many other British towns. Haberdasheries, ironmongers, knitting shops and gentleman's outfitters are still to be found among the newer arrivals alongside the ubiquitous high street brands.

If you prefer paying more for old clothes than you would new clothes, then the town's thriving **Vintage Retro Boho-Chic Stuff Your Gran Threw Out 40 Years Ago As Worthless** scene will leave you spoilt for choice, but careful scrutiny is advised if you are looking for the genuine article. Many of the town's 63,000 charity shops' retro rails have allegedly also been known to ship in reproduction vintage from China, so if you are seeking genuine stains in the armpits of wide-collared blouses or yellowing in the crotches of old crimplene suits, be sure to ask the provenance of the outfit.

If you still have the energy after walking the length of the High Street, the indoor **Whitstable Swimming Pool**, located near the EAST QUAY, is a good alternative to the sea, especially on days when strong currents form a foaming white residue upon the shoreline. So as not to disappoint the visitor who may have been looking forward to a bracing dip in the sea, the temperature of the indoor pool is allegedly maintained at the same seasonal temperature as the sea year-round, and has the added bonus that one need not be constantly on guard for the infamous Crabzilla.

If you are feeling hungry, the town offers many options, from locally high-end seafood restaurants to the more traditional, and fish and chip shops such as **Ron's Plaice**. If unidentified compressed meat is your preference, you won't be disappointed by the numerous **kebab shops** that allegedly sell this fine fare and are dotted around the town, although sachets of ketchup are not always available.

For something more bijou, try the great selection of charcuteries and organic cafés for which the town has become famous in recent decades. **Swindler's** is allegedly one of the best and offers artisan breads, wheat-grass smoothies, detoxifying cabbage soup, rainforest-friendly salami and King Cobra cheese direct from Uzbekistan. For the price of a laden shopping trolley at Aldi, delicious sandwiches garnished with a slither of lettuce and half a tomato served can be had, and of course, like many other eating establishments in the town, all are guaranteed to come served with sachets of appetising sauces including the ever-popular ketchup and the noble brown.

On a night time the town's pubs and bars offer a range of drinks not dissimilar to London prices. This has the double bonus of offering the visitor a London experience without having to make the journey to the capital.

If you are looking for a fight, the visitor will be disappointed if they visit the town during the mid-week as tempers outside the pubs and bars tend to occur more usually on Friday and Saturday evenings after closing time. The more reliable option is to take the short trip to nearby HERNE BAY anytime during the week but be prepared to pay less for drinks.

Similarly, accommodation can vary depending on your budget. The playfully-named **Sock Under the Bed** guest house, just off the High Street, is a good choice for those looking for a traditional British post-war B&B experience.

As the name suggests, stray socks lightly covered in dust can always be found beneath the beds at no extra charge and nylon bed sheets are always guaranteed. Each room comes equipped with tea and coffee making facilities and both hot AND cold running water. Breakfasts are a hearty affair here. The Traditional English, a cornucopia of fried pig products, comes served with the town's best selection of sachets of ketchup and brown sauce for a modest surcharge, spoonfuls of extra grease are complimentary and the front door stays conveniently unlocked until 10.15 each evening.

GETTING THERE

The town is well connected by mainline trains and the beautiful Thanet Way dual carriageway. If arriving by car please do remember to check your bank balance in advance as local councillors have ensured parking charges are creatively priced. If you wish to arrive as one might have done in centuries past, the **Crab and Winkle Way**, which runs through the ancient **Forest of Blean** to CANTERBURY, is an exciting way to approach the town. Unlike the town's beach hut areas, the bridle path along the Way allegedly offers a far higher incidence of being murdered, but has the added benefit of not being crowded by hundreds of detective-murder amateur writers looking to set their stories here, most notably the **Writers of Whitstable** group.

The Pink Glove

by Laura Sehjal

Only the thumb and first finger were currently visible. Jemma wanted to reach out and touch its soft leather as soon as it caught her eye, but couldn't get to it because of all the rubbish piled up in the living room. She couldn't even see the floor.

How had her mother been living like this? How had she not known? The guilt crept up her neck and flushed her face. She angled her body so that The Neighbour couldn't see the shock and embarrassment written all over her. She wished she were alone to take this in properly.

'So, as you can probably smell,' The Neighbour was saying, 'it's really bad in here. It's driving me insane. It's all I can smell in my hallway. Something has to be done about it and now that your mum has passed...'

The Neighbour trailed off whilst avoiding eye contact. She must think that I'm the worst daughter ever, thought Jemma. Faced with the reality of how her mum had been living, she would have to agree with her, but in her defence she'd had the worst mother ever. The Neighbour hadn't done anything about that either.

Jemma nodded, but had no idea what she was going to do about the smell, the rubbish, the house. What could she do about it from London? She could pay someone to come and sort it all but...

A silence filled the air that seemed to stretch and expand

as Jemma took in the gravity of what she was facing and The Neighbour analysed Jemma's reaction to the house out of the corner of her eye; judgement emanating from her very core.

'Right,' said The Neighbour eventually, 'I'll leave you to make a start. I'll just be next door if you need anything.'

The Neighbour took one last sweeping look around the living room, stuck her nose in the air and left. The front door clicked shut.

Standing alone in the vast remains of her mother's life seemed to suck the air out of the room along with Jemma's resolve. She sank to her knees, resting them on a pile of books, and stared into space.

Somewhere in a dark corner, in the dusty depths of her memory, images and sounds began to stir and resurface that she had worked so hard to repress. Images of her abusive childhood that she had, until this very moment, successfully muted with expensive rugs, a bespoke kitchen, and a solid career in advertising that took every waking thought she had.

Jemma's subconscious mind inadvertently conjured up the distant bang of a door and the chunter of her mother's daily ramblings. The sound of her school friends sniggering and laughing at having seen her mother rummaging in bins to collect and recycle discarded plastic for the sculpture she insisted she was working on. Art projects, paintings, scraps of non-sensical ideas on bits of paper found hidden deep in the breakfast cereal boxes, 'So they couldn't be stolen,' her mother used to inform her. 'Artistic copyright is a hard one to enforce – better to protect your ideas from the off.'

Her mother had always been messy, dirty, a collector, but never this bad. Clean bedding and hoovering had been a rarity in Jemma's childhood, but the dirt present here now beggared belief. The whole room seemed to be covered in a thick film of grime that clung to any and every exposed surface. The stacks of magazines, books and boxes, teetering in unstable towers, seemed to be closing in on her, threatening to come crashing down any moment.

A memory of a slap echoed across Jemma's cheek. A voice

bubbled up telling her that she would never become anything – no resolve. A push, a sly nip. 'Knock you down so I can build you up.' 'All that success you've had – because of me that is. Do you ever thank me? Do you ever even come to see me?'

Angry tears stung her eyes as she tried to take a lungful of dust filled air. Unable to stand the feeling of being stifled in that house any longer, Jemma waded through piles of paper, kicking over boxes en route to the window, spilling their banal contents onto yet more rubbish. She struggled with the filth-filled mechanism on the sash window, but eventually managed to throw it open.

Amazing salty sea air hit Jemma's lungs. It had the calming effect that it always had done. She closed her eyes and allowed herself to breathe. She'd stopped being able to see any beauty in Whitstable a long time ago, but she'd never forgotten the soothing influence of the sea: her only friend and confidant during her formative years.

She turned back to the interior of the house with new resolve and stormed into the hall, grabbed one of the bin bags out of her cleaning box, and realised that the products she'd brought with her were woefully insufficient to deal with the task at hand. Nevertheless, Jemma put on a pair of marigolds and hoped that they would provide some meagre protection from whatever she was about to find buried beneath these piles.

'Start in a corner and just work methodically outwards,' she said to herself. 'Don't look, just bin. Grab. Toss.'

Jemma's instant reaction was to make a beeline for the pink glove she'd seen earlier, partially covered. But she restrained herself and bent down where she was to begin.

A broken doll that looked suspiciously like her childhood doll, Rosie… only with an eye, arm and most of her hair missing.

Bin.

A pile of magazines from the 1990s cataloguing the life of bugs and insects (Jemma had once had a fascination with ladybirds and beetles).

Bin.

Toffee tins, old milk cartons, toy cars, teddies with heads hanging on by a thread.

Bin. Bin. Bin.

She was on a roll now.

She powered through old bills, old Christmas cards, boxes that had been empty for decades.

Penguin books, Enid Blyton books, Roald Dahl books – they had all been on her bedroom shelf once upon a time.

Jemma tried to push the question of how they had made their way downstairs from her mind, because the sadness that welled up inside when she thought of her mum treasuring her discarded possessions kept threatening to erupt at any minute. She carried on, reminding herself that it was a shame her mum could never show her daughter the same affection that she had shown inanimate objects.

A desperate loneliness emanated from each object that Jemma touched. They all seemed lost, completely without meaning or context amongst the horde of other apparently random items. Jostling for their place in the world but finally resigning themselves to their fate here in this house. Archived and treasured by someone who, for some reason, had seen meaning in them.

Jemma supposed that her mother had also been a bit of a lost soul. Unable to show affection or empathise with other people's emotions, she had slowly shut herself off from the outside world; taking her anger out more and more often on Jemma.

Three hours later Jemma peeled off her marigolds and glanced at her watch. She was exhausted. Looking around the room she realised that she had subconsciously cleared a path that led back to the pink glove. She bent down to pick it up and throw it in the bin bag when she paused. Something about the coolness against her skin jarred her.

The gloves had been the only gift that she had ever willingly given to her mum. On a rare visit from London Jemma had presented them to her, hand-wrapped in fragile tissue paper.

When she'd seen them in the shop she could just imagine her mum wearing them as they had seemed slightly eccentric somehow. A wave of guilt had flooded over her and she'd made the purchase to try and quell it.

Her mum had torn through the tissue paper and then promptly tossed them on the floor with a torrent of abuse about how *things* weren't going to make Jemma any less of an insignificant person in her life. Jemma clung on to this hurt whenever she felt guilty about not seeing her mother in the future.

She slipped her hand inside the glove and flexed her fingers, taking in the brightness of the pink. She looked around for its pair but couldn't see it anywhere.

Upon closer examination Jemma could see there was a snag on the edge of the little finger where it had presumably caught on something sharp. 'She wore this after all,' thought Jemma. 'To snag this, she *must* have worn it.' She held the glove to her cheek and imagined her Mum's hand encasing hers in a way that it never had done in life. There was nothing particularly special about this glove if she was honest, no more special than the rest of the junk in this room that her mother had touched; yet she couldn't help but be drawn to it and couldn't explain it either.

She picked up a framed picture of a dog that Jemma had drawn when she was a young teenager, and wiped some of the dust from the frame. Something else that her mum had preserved.

With a sigh Jemma put the picture frame in the bin bag. 'No use in hanging on to the past. Let go and move forward,' she told herself firmly. She began to peel the glove from her hand one finger at a time. She was just about to drop it in the bin bag when there was a knock at the door and The Neighbour's head popped round the corner.

'You're still here then? Thought I'd see if you want a cuppa.'

'No, I'm fine. Thank you,' replied Jemma curtly. 'I'm going to call it a day.'

Almost without thinking Jemma picked up her handbag, slipped the pink glove safely inside and pushed past The Neighbour into the refreshing Whitstable air.

Moved

by John Wilkins

So I've moved. Ninety-five years and gone – passed on. Now I'm the late Winona Rose Williams. I was remembering when we took the three of them on a day out to Whitstable. Then I was moved – you aren't expected to say died – and I can watch everyone until my funeral and then that's it, I'm gone. That's all I've been told and this is what I watched.

When I saw them, they always made me realise how different each of them was. Now I'm *gone*, looking down on them I can see something of me in all of them. I believe that a part of me will live on in each of them, my children. I hope the worst parts of me don't continue though. I probably caused a lot more trouble than I should have done.

There's my eldest now, Tom. I can see my wish has been granted – to find him straight away. He's behaving exactly as I thought he would. I can hear myself talking to him as he grew up, when he told me about what he had decided, about who and what he wanted to be. It was always what I had hoped for, and just proved that all the worrying I did – about whether or not he would be able to be what he wanted to be – had been a big waste of time. But that was always the case. 'I might have known' was what I usually told myself when things turned out all right in the end for Tom, as they usually did.

He's putting the telephone down now and telling Jacqueline, his wife. She's hardly awake. Tom was the morning man – off to do his paper round without ever needing an alarm clock to wake him. She's awake now, I can see by the way she is looking at his face. He must be telling her about me. I can't hear where I am but I'm guessing she's saying something about 'They were expecting it any time soon with her being ninety-five.' She's moved and sat up now on the bed. She's put her arms up to him and he sits down next to her and turns into her. So she wakes up looking as good as that, does she? Well I'll give her credit – there aren't many women who can manage it! At least I can understand properly what he saw in her now, finally. Mind you, she did try very hard with me, even though I think she could tell straight away that I didn't think she was good enough for him, not my Tom, the firstborn.

He looks all right at the moment, and I think he knew at any rate, that it wouldn't be long, before I was *gone*. Tom used to come and see me every Sunday, brought the children with him too. That last Sunday he looked at me and said 'Take care of yourself, Mum.' I felt strange too as I watched him turn and smile back at me, his slim shape framed in the doorway of my room in the care home.

Jacqueline's listening to Tom now. She's standing up, going to the end of the bed and pulling on that dressing gown I bought for her last Christmas. Huh, no more shopping trips for me now. She's nodding her head while he talks to her, as he puts slippers on his feet. I expect he'll pull himself together after he's had a cup of coffee. That's what they drink – you wouldn't believe it would you, not after being brought up in a home where there was always a pot of tea ready-made.

I want to see what the other two are up to now. I expect the youngest, my daughter Tina, will be in a state. She'll probably have a fag, and that mascara she's plastered on her face since she was a teenager will be all over the place. There isn't much space for her in that little council house, not for her to hide herself away until she's sorted herself out. At least they own it – which is a miracle when you think about it, with her Derek always being in and out of work. He changed jobs more often than the weather, did Derek. Then Tina had her illness – it was just a procedure, she told me – but I knew what that was about. That was all down to the smoking, but you don't say anything, do you. So she never went back to work after that. She looked after the twins Sue and Sam. They were a handful too. Both of them calmed down when they got older, just proper surly teenagers like their mother used to be. Oh how I laughed when she used to tell me how moody they were. Now you know what it's like, I thought, what you put me and your father through.

The four of them are sitting down at the table, in the kitchen he 'built the extension onto' so that the tumble dryer and the washing machine 'had enough space' as Derek put it. Well I never, that's a sight I've never seen before – Derek with his arm round Tina. Mind you, she is in a state and now the kids too. Sue gets up and rushes to hold her too and Sam doesn't look like he's too happy either. Mind you, he's not known for being the life and soul of the party. Tina stands up and walks out of the kitchen. Oh, she's going to the telephone – she's running to it like I remember seeing her do. When I was younger, I went round on a Wednesday – it broke the week up. She told me how the kids were doing at school, what she planned for Christmas, that sort of thing. I didn't pay much attention, it was just about keeping in touch. I kept my distance after the way she left home. That left a deep scar, that did. She's holding the telephone away from her head and I can tell by the way her shoulders are going up and down she's getting more upset. It's probably Aaron trying to find out what's going on. Tom would have called him and broken the news.

I don't know how Aaron would have taken it. I could never read Aaron like I could the other two. He mystified me, that one. I never knew how he was going to turn out. To tell the truth, I didn't find out for a long time, either. He got himself a job and paid his way though. He did something with telephones, some sort of engineering, I think. Yes, come to think of it, he would turn up out of the blue and take me out to lunch, especially after I was moved into the care home. 'You need to go out for a bite to eat, Mum,' he would say and it wasn't an invitation, it was a statement of fact. I said to him once, 'What if I told you "*No* I'm busy" when you just turn up like this?' Aaron flew off the handle at me, swore black and blue that he had phoned me the previous week and I'd agreed. Well I couldn't remember so I had to give him the benefit of the doubt. Maybe my memory had got worse. I suppose it does when you're getting on a bit. Then I started writing it down in a diary – it gave me something to look forward to. You can go stir crazy sometimes with just those four walls to look at. Those care homes were all the same.

There's Aaron, he's walking in a park or somewhere. He's holding his hand to his ear. I know what that means – it's the mobile phone. He's upset and his arms are waving about as if the person he's talking to can see how bad he's feeling. I wish I could get on these telephone calls and tell them I'm all right but you can't. It isn't allowed, apparently. I suppose because you could drive people mad – they would think they were hearing voices. Of course you could say you wanted to change your mind about the will, the funeral, and get up to all sorts of mischief. I didn't leave much – it all went on the care homes really, when I think back. I had those policies that pay out after you've gone. Tom had power of attorney and dealt with that side of things so I don't need to worry that I left a mess behind to sort out.

I just want to say goodbye and leave something for them to remember me by. I suppose they will remember me. I hope I'll remember them wherever I'm moving to after the funeral. I'm not sure I want to see any more. Yes, just Tom. If I can see what he's up to now and how he's coping then I know the other two will follow him. It's certainly different to what I imagined. Nothing like the films – with the gravestone and everyone in the graveyard standing round it. I'm having the cremation anyway. Still, there will be a plaque next to my husband in the crematorium, with my name on it. Winona Rose Williams.

Winona – everybody called me *Win* as soon as I went to school. The name my parents chose because it couldn't be shortened like Sue or Sam. So I was *Win* for most of my life. I remember my husband's joke about it the day we were married. After our names were read out in the church I think he knew I would always be *Win*. After all it was him who said, 'it has a very positive ring to it,' and we both laughed; and I kept the photograph of us laughing outside the church on our wedding day, by my side of the bed.

So I'm trying to see Tom and it is harder to do now but yes I can make him out, and Jacqueline. They are standing outside a bungalow with a *For Sale* sign. There's a boy in a suit with them and both Tom and Jacqueline are shaking hands with him. They're going up the drive together and the boy in the suit goes in first. Then the boy in the suit comes out with a man holding a notepad or something. They shake hands and the older man walks down the drive and then turns up the road to a van with Builders in huge letters printed across the rear doors.

The boy has gone back in. I wait. If they're moving, then where are Tom and Jacqueline moving to? Where is this place, I think, and then look at the sign to make out Whitstable at the bottom of it under what must be the estate agent's name. Are they moving to Whitstable?

The boy comes out of the bungalow first – he pulls a phone out and then talks with it in front of his face as if he can see who is on the line – perhaps you can do that these days. He's laughing and nodding his head. Then he puts the phone back inside his jacket. He leans against the fence that edges the little front garden – well, little compared to what we used to have. Here's Tom and now Jacqueline. Tom looks at Jacqueline with that face that I know means 'you will agree with me,' and they both turn to the boy and start talking at him. The boy holds both his hands up – I think he's trying to get them to stop talking. He reaches inside his jacket and brings out the phone. This time he taps the screen then he holds it to his ear. He holds his hand up to stop Jacqueline talking. Tom turns her away and walks to the end of the drive where there is a garage. They turn and go towards a side entrance but the boy runs towards them and he's laughing and giving his hand to Tom who shakes it. Tom turns to Jacqueline and she throws her head back and then she kisses him and the boy too. The boy looks very pleased – he must have sold them the place. They start to walk back down the drive and when they reach the end of it the hand shaking starts again. Tom and the boy nod at each other.

Jacqueline is walking back to their car then she stops – she's seen something – it's a street sign. I doubt I'll recognise where we are – the furthest we explored was to find that amazing chip shop on the Tankerton high road. I can see the sign now that Tom has moved her back and is pointing to the name and then he holds her. The name of the road is Good*win* Avenue. So this is how they will remember me. I am as moved to find my name as they are.

Whitstable Parking is on the Agenda

By Joanne Bartley

I was thrilled to win the election. People simply put a cross beside any candidate wearing the right colour rosette, but 2,222 of those crosses were for me. The number felt magical. I knew better than most that it wasn't magical at all. My maths teacher explained patternicity long ago. The other boys would seek out a face in a picture of tree bark. I would see the human tendency to make sense from randomness. Magic was something very different.

Those 2,222 people didn't know my name. They didn't know anything about me, and they couldn't know the real me. If they did I felt sure I would win more votes. I hoped one day they would have reason to talk about me.

The emails and phone calls were never ending. Pavement holes. Bins. Parking. Always the parking! Traffic chaos in the summer brought the town to a standstill. Tourists were frustrated and locals fussed when there was no space for a car beside their Victorian terrace.

It seemed nothing could be done. The town was simply too small for all the cars. The people who desired period fireplaces and cornices also wanted the modern perks of driveways and garages.

Committees debated, consultations were proposed, traffic

experts gave their views. Mrs Baker of Nelson Road asked me why nothing was done about the double yellow lines. Bill from the chip shop complained about his loading bay.

I devised a standard email reply. It had the right tone of sympathy and offered an upbeat suggestion that this issue was being reviewed. Something would be done soon. That's what it said.

But it would only get done if someone decided to take this on. I am a practical person, and an unusual one. I wanted to make a difference.

The idea came to me during a Planning Committee meeting.

It frustrated me that people could only argue against a development by reference to the materials or building height. Not, 'Nobody likes it, it's ugly.'

The worst developers would submit 100 page reports with 30 or more attachments. How could any member of the public argue with that, or even find time to read it all? Council officers would advise 'That's not admissible as grounds for an objection' as a dear old lady would cry, 'But I've lived here thirty years!' There would be a skim read of the key points, a few questions asked, then with a sense of defeat the bad plans would be approved.

There was too much talk and a lack of sensible action. In most cases there was no action at all.

My idea grew in the Policy and Resources meeting.

New legislation was discussed; this gave the council new powers to create any business venture. Any money made would help the council's budget. Local government cuts were on the cards and entrepreneurial councils were to be applauded. The Marlowe Theatre was discussed as an example of a council business. It didn't make much money, but everyone chatted about their favourite shows, and someone pointed out that there were reduced price tickets to the civic performance of the pantomime.

Councillor Barton proposed renting out student housing. Councillor Clegg objected because her husband ran a student letting company. I let them debate as I sat quietly, thinking of my parking plan. I liked my idea better the more I thought about it.

I sent my proposal to the Property and Regeneration officers the very next day. Of course I knew this would be a lengthy process with reports and many meetings. I was right, my plan would be discussed in a meeting scheduled for June. Then the meeting was cancelled because the Joint Transportation Board was rearranged. I turned page after page in my diary and despaired.

But I had other ways to do things. I could make things happen my own way.

I made an excuse to visit the council planning department.

The council officer blinked a few times, stuttered mid-sentence, and said, 'That sounds like a marvellous idea, let's give it a go! I'll sort the admin side, leave it with me.'

Parking In The Sky Enterprises was founded. The car park near the Horsebridge Centre was the first site. It seemed a shame that the cars in the Island Wall car park had such lovely sea views. Cars didn't need sea views – people did. So we located the first Car Park In The Sky in the air above the beach. We turned the former car park into a garden with benches and a wooden sculpture tide clock.

The Gorrell Tank car park was costly to repair and likely to be closed for many months, but it took only a moment to create unlimited parking in the clouds above its concrete. I had a dental appointment the next day and smiled at the overhead photo of Whitstable pinned above the dentist's chair. I knew it was designed to distract me from fingers in my mouth, and it did distract me, because I lay there and imagined a new town growing in the sky above the ceiling.

The tourists loved my car parks. Whitstable Castle was particularly busy when I planted a car park above the gardens. You could buy a cream tea in the Orangery and watch the cars get sucked into the air and then vanish six feet up.

I decided to make the cars turn invisible at around head

height because it was neater. No one wanted to see traffic congestion in the air.

The town was packed at weekends, and this normally caused traffic gridlock. But there was no need for a Whitstable Park and Ride scheme. I created a car park in the sky above the Two Brewers pub at the bottom of Borstal Hill. The Chamber of Commerce loved this because tourists would explore the unfashionable end of town. The pub found new trade selling postcards of flying cars alongside their beer and beverages.

The people kept coming. So another parking place was proposed. The councillors from the Planning Committee wanted to hold a public consultation. They hoped to find a suitable site and then seek approval through the planning application process.

I didn't think an invisible car park needed a planning application. What would the application document say? Dimensions: 0 feet. Building materials: None. This was hardly a cause for public objections.

So I avoided the fuss and created a new invisible parking spot, siting it in Tankerton near the roundabout. I was friendly with Henry from the wine shop and I thought he'd like a car park a few thousand feet above his shop.

The cars flew high, but I decided to keep my head down. It took only a moment to magic up the car parks. I spent much longer on my regular council business. Serco emptied the Clare Road bins late two weeks in a row so I got a lot of emails. It was satisfying helping people, but a lot of work.

I ran into the Council Leader at the reception after the civic performance of the Marlowe pantomime. James was a bright young chap, but he looked flustered.

'Did you like the show?' I asked.

'Oh yes, but I've just had a call from the Director of Resources.'

A pantomime dame in a three foot wide dress approached, wobbling, with a drink in hand. The Dame grasped our esteemed leader's hand. 'So very thrilled to meet you!' He, or she, batted her eyes in a comedic fashion.

'Lovely... Great show,' James said.

I could see James didn't want to talk. I helped him with a magical moment and the Dame went on his, or her, way.

'Oh, is there some trouble for our officers?'

'Oh no. Quite the opposite. We've been offered rather a lot of money for the Parking In The Sky to expand.'

'Oh, the parking does seem quite popular.' I was quietly pleased. I rarely received praise for my council work. I was not one to brag but I did think my car parks were quite good.

'Yes.' James frowned and then laughed. 'It's a crazy amount of money. New York want them, Singapore too... And Canada, what's the capital of Canada? Doesn't matter! All these huge cities want Whitstable parking!'

'Oh.' I wasn't keen to travel the world. But I was the only one who could put car parks in the sky.

'It's all fine, we should take the money... but the council officers are being funny about trade secrets and "implementation concerns". Whatever that means.'

I had concerns about the implementation too. I wondered if I could use Google Maps and look at Singapore streets then build an invisible sky car park somehow. I had no desire to leave my comfortable home on Cromwell Road.

'Damn it! We can't turn that money down.' Simon took his mobile out of his pocket. He downed his wine and looked ready for business. 'Look, Rupert, say yes. Add another zero for the implementation issues, they'll pay. At that price we need to expand Car Parks In The Sky worldwide!'

I had a queasy feeling, and it was not the post-show canapes. I felt peculiar because I hadn't signed up as a councillor to create car parks in faraway foreign cities. I just wanted to serve my community, to help the people of Whitstable. I was already concerned because I had several emails from a resident on Castle Road. I'd kept him waiting two days already. If I was setting up car parks in New York, my council work would suffer. Mr Richards wanted assistance with setting up a Neighbourhood Watch Scheme in his road. If I helped him I would feel far more satisfied than if I flew cars to the Ottowan clouds.

James put the phone down and looked satisfied. 'This is quite a life changer,' he said. He grasped my shoulders firmly. 'Your Whitstable folks should be very happy indeed.'

I didn't understand what he meant until a few months later. The global expansion of Car Parks In The Sky was approved unanimously in the Policy & Resources meeting. There were cheers when the financial details were read out. The opposition councillor asked for a report assessing potential pollution, but we had a majority of twenty-one and nothing she said was ever considered.

I made a note to look into magically eliminating car emissions, but it would be added to a rather busy To Do list. When the meeting finished I went home and checked the report for the locations of the faraway car parks. The Google Map idea worked, so I set them up and went to bed.

The Chief Executive of Canterbury City Council was quoted in Thursday's Whitstable Gazette saying, 'The worldwide expansion of our car park venture is not only the most valuable council deal I've ever made, but also the smoothest business transaction.'

It turned out the ten billion cash injection did make Whitstable folk happy. We couldn't charge council tax any more. There was so much money in the council accounts we had to pay residents who lived in the Canterbury district.

Mr Roberts of Castle Road wrote a nice email thanking me for helping with the Neighbourhood Watch scheme. He pointed out that local people were now so wealthy the risk of petty crime must be much reduced.

Many people gave up work when they received the Canterbury City Council bonus. I noticed the difference in the High Street when I shopped. People had more time to stop and say hello. I encouraged people to get involved with a few of my favourite projects. I organised a beach clean and eighteen people helped out!

There were a few negatives to the car park deal; house prices went up significantly. Down From Londoners (DFL) used to move to town and buy houses, but they could no longer afford to live in the area. Many Whitstable residents bought second homes in the capital and were known as Locals Owning London (LOLs). It was understandable that everyone wanted to live in the Canterbury City Council District due to the residents' bonus, and also because the area was pleasingly free of parking problems. Whitstable was much sought after, obviously the best town in the area.

No one minded that DFL were priced out of the housing market, but it was a problem when local families couldn't afford to buy houses either. There was only one answer. We needed Houses in the Sky.

The council house waiting list revealed that 3,507 families needed accommodation, so I created 3,507 houses in the clouds above Whitstable. The children were very excited about being teleported.

I made the way up and down near the war memorial. Brian from the Chamber of Commerce and I agreed that this end of town suited locals better than Harbour Street. I was a regular shopper at the larger Co Op myself. I decided the new tenants would need a supermarket far more than boutique clothes or cupcakes. Not that I had anything against cupcakes, and the Whitstable Produce Store's Kentinental breakfast always made me laugh with its witty name.

The houses in the sky were popular. The people living there became known as Down From Skys, or DFS, just like the sofa shops.

People enjoyed their new homes, which had sea views most of the time, depending on the cloud cover. I knew I had to expand the sky community to meet increasing demand so I sited another 1,000 houses up there to be sold as affordable homes.

I created a new way up and down beside the playground in Cornwallis Circle, and the children liked that. I expanded the up and down paths to a few more places, even one going to Whats Up Cupcake, because with so much disposable income no one seemed to mind paying £2 for cake.

The town grew ever upwards, it was far higher and more prosperous than it had ever been before. As a member of the Whitstable Society I was sensitive to concerns that the historic character of the town should be preserved. A few people campaigned to remove the ugly tower block near Belmont Road so I re-sited that three thousand feet upwards. Then a local group successfully crowdfunded to buy the aggregates factory. The ugly grey building was vaporised and replaced with a coastal park. Someone suggested the wind farms were an eye sore too, but the Green Party wrote letters about renewable energy hoping to keep them. I considered giving Whitstable unlimited electric power, but I rather liked seeing the wind turbines out at sea so I didn't bother.

Things were going rather well, and I was looking forward to a bit of leafleting with the local elections coming up. The mood of the people was chipper, and people liked Canterbury City Council for making them all wealthy with no need to work. I hoped to increase my majority and avoid nips by dogs when I posted my flyers into letter boxes.

I was pleased that Mr Roberts of Castle Road was standing as an Independent candidate. He'd shown good initiative with his Neighbourhood Watch scheme, and even though we were rivals for the ward seat I gave him a lift to the count on election day.

The tellers piled ballot papers up, checking the cross beside each candidate's name then sorting the papers. I could see that Mr Roberts was doing rather well. His Neighbourhood Watch scheme was well liked and people knew his name. I'd even helped him set up a crime prevention plan in our area; in the event of any crime it suspended crooks in mid-air until the police arrived.

No one knew my name, but that didn't worry me. I wore my usual rosette, and I trusted people to note the colour and vote in the usual way.

As the papers piled higher I could see that Mr Roberts was ahead of me in the count. I thought of building my pile of ballot papers so high that they reached the car parks and houses in the sky... Of course rigging an election with magic was completely unethical. So I had to accept that this was not my day. My life as a Canterbury City Council councillor was over.

I shook Mr Roberts' hand. 'Well done, you'll make a fine councillor!'

He seemed stunned by his victory.

'Don't worry, it's all good fun, and your Neighbourhood Watch experience will stand you in good stead. The people have made their choice.'

Mr Roberts said he was honoured and wished me well for the future. I didn't wait for the official announcement as the result was clear. To be honest I was a little flustered, though I don't usually get emotional.

I was ready for a new phase of my life. I was sailing past flying cars, soaring beyond the cloud houses, whizzing past the teleporting kiddies heading to the playground.

I couldn't stay in Whitstable. I couldn't be there when the people needed houses. I couldn't stand to see all the traffic needing parking. I wouldn't know what to do with myself when Serco were late on recycling bins day.

So I flew high out over the sea. I flew as far and as fast as I could.

I had a few regrets. I would miss sending emails to help people. I would miss the letters Cllr after my name. My Community College in the Clouds would never teach high flying students. But the people had made a choice. I respected the role of democracy, even though it hurt me cruelly.

My new home had a view of the spinning wind turbines. The concrete and beams of the Maunsell Forts offered solitude. I'd always admired these funny lumps of metal, legs splayed like rusty robots striding across the sea.

I created an interconnecting invisible passage to connect the old towers. I laid a Persian rug in my hallway, a bit like the one my mother used to have. The gun terrace made a pleasing balcony. My deckchair was comfortable and I could sit and watch Whitstable from afar. I threw a biscuit to a passing seagull and it caught it with a mid-air gulp. I listened to the waves and enjoyed a cup of tea.

The cars started falling at dusk, crashing and splashing into the sea. There was a distant clang when they hit the pebbles of the beach.

I was sad not to be involved with the Joint Transportation Board any more, but the new elected representatives were all very capable. There would be a spring in the step of each new councillor. It was a time for new blood and they would tackle things their own way.

The crashes came every few minutes and the horns and sirens were non-stop, but I made sure the raining cars didn't hurt anyone. There would be many cars with nowhere to park, but this was no longer my responsibility.

The houses in the clouds started to disintegrate and the people tumbled out of the doors, falling with flapping arms to land beside the war memorial, the playground and the cupcake shop. These people would need new homes, but I was reassured that a house move could be a positive. My new place out at sea was a big improvement on my Cromwell Road flat. Mr Roberts was their elected representative now, and he was very conscientious. I was sure their new neighbourhoods would be safe.

Whitstable parking would be back on the agenda. New faces on the committees, a fresh email response to parking concerns.

I poured another cup of tea and stirred in the sugar. I watched the sun set and realised it was the first time I'd seen a sunset properly for years. My new life was starting. It felt magical.

The Olive Branch

By James Dutch

On the third morning, in the slatted light of the patient's room, two men sat waiting for a sign: the flicker of an eyelid, a breath that was deeper or shallower than the one that preceded it. The thin man stood and walked quietly to the window, beckoned by a cacophony of gulls screeching outside. He peered through the gaps of the venetian blind and squinted, the intense brightness of the early summer sun reflecting off the calm sea as it tenderly kissed the shore under the green fringe of the slopes. The gulls, lazing upon thermals, cried again, a wretched sound that echoed his heart. Bringing the patient here to the large private house had been the only thing they'd agreed on, to get her away from London to her childhood holiday destination where the sea air and fond memories would do her good. The fat man didn't like it here. The air was too dry and the rain was too wet. But the thin man knew the benefits; was aware of the good health and longevity of the local residents. He pulled at his tie and loosened the collar of his shirt, pulling the material away from his damp skin. The fat man sitting silently, sweating, winced in disgust at the noise of the finger brushing the starched cotton. He closed his eyes and shuddered as though someone had stepped on his grave before returning his longing gaze to the patient.

The first two days in the house together had been war. Arguments, shouting, accusations, and blame being thrown, jabbed and sliced. The fat man would attack first, without provocation. 'How could you do it? You betrayed me!' His stubby fingers jabbed towards the thin man, but he never actually touched him, alert to the fact that once he made physical contact he might not be able to stop.

The thin man would counter with a precisely aimed volley. 'If you'd spent less time on the golf course and more time at home, this would never have happened.'

'*My* fault!' The fat man would be incredulous, shaking his head at the nerve.

The Doctor had insisted that they would have to leave the room if they did not call an immediate ceasefire. And now instead of being full of shouts and bitter words, the air became thick, pulsing with the silence of unspoken recriminations, rages and regrets.

On the fourth day the two men reached an uneasy truce, a politeness for the sake of the patient. 'Look at this.' The thin man held open the newspaper. 'The world's first transmission of colour television. Do you think it'll catch on?' As an astute businessman in the industry with a nose for success, he knew the answer already, but he needed to engage his friend on old terms, familiar terms, before all was lost.

The fat man huffed as he struggled to lean forward to read the article. 'Talkies look like they're going to catch on,' he said flatly. 'I don't see why colour won't.' Sighing, the fat man sat back in his chair and wiped at his small moustache. He could sense his old friend attempting to build a bridge, and he loved and hated him for it. Wished he would go away, but wanted him to stay if only to make sure he was suffering too.

'Just imagine it, not just talkies, but movies in colour, too!' The thin man, always eager for new opportunities, attempted a smile, folded the newspaper and sat forward in his chair. 'Let's not give it all up. What do you say?' The fat man raised a questioning eyebrow. 'We were like brothers! Nothing could come between us,' the thin man in his tweed suit said. He knew he had to try harder than the fat man dressed in blue serge.

'Brothers don't do that,' replied the fat man, looking away, and he was right. Each time he felt the thin man reach out to him, he would begin to warm before the tendrils of icy bitterness wrapped themselves around his heart and the silence would return.

That afternoon, the thin man was allowed to visit the second patient, which he began to do regularly and without telling the fat man where he was going, or where he had been. The fat man had no interest in the second patient, and barely registered the weak cry she made when she needed attention. His whole world was hanging in the balance before him.

After six days the fat man no longer cared to ask the other whether he too wanted refreshment when visiting the scullery or ringing for the maid. The years of being friends, being *like brothers*, the long road trodden to becoming the most successful double act in the golden age of film, were forgotten. But now, like an old married couple that no longer loved each other but to whom the thought of separating was akin to losing a limb, they sat in regretful silence. All that kept them in the same room now was the first patient, and Hollywood was far behind them. The Doctor's visits were becoming more frequent and even more discouraging.

Ten days into the vigil and each man no longer saw the other, like a shadow in his armchair on either side of the bed. The weather had not delivered a sea breeze in days and the fat man, close to melting, fanned himself with a three month old issue of *Variety*, the headline TRY TO SAVE THE DRAMA flapped rhythmically into his vision. The thin man in tweed sat still, his pale hands held in his lap, until he paid a visit to the second patient, answering the thin mewling noise she made when the nurse didn't come quickly enough. He was allowed to take her for a walk outside, and headed westward along the top of the slopes. The fat man peered out of the window, grief stricken to see the other half of his world strolling along Marine Parade and down to the sea where the tide shushed at the ladies and children splashing and laughing. His thick fingers hurriedly pulled at the cord of the blind bringing it slicing down like a guillotine, cutting him off from the everyday life outside. He choked back a sob and pressed his finger and thumb to his eyes, pinching the bridge of his nose to prevent the tears.

On the morning of the eleventh day, the patient's eyes fluttered open. The fat man stood suddenly and threw himself at his wife's bedside. The thin man gripped the arms of his chair and slowly pushed himself towards standing, and then sat down again after a warning glance was shot his way. The fat man's wife smiled at him, attempted words, and then drew her last breath. The thin man, his cheeks wet and salty as though the tide had lapped his face, turned his back on the devastation and left the room to visit the second patient. The fat man, down on one knee like the day he proposed, howled.

As the thin man held the second patient in his arms, he listened to the steadily decreasing sobs from across the corridor and lamented the loss of the fat man's wife. They had both loved her, but it was his love which had created this child, and therefore his love that had led to her passing away from the puerperal fever she developed during childbirth. Now a piece of her lived on through this helpless innocent he cradled, and yet the fat man did not want to acknowledge its existence.

As the fat man held his wife in his arms, he cried. He cried at the loss of his dear wife, he cried at the loss of a dear friend, and he cried because he would never know his wife's only child, the child that should have been his. And even though the thin man would hold an olive branch out toward him for the rest of his days, he would never be able to accept it. How could he even set eyes upon the murderous child and its accessory father? The Doctor arrived, confirmed the death and covered the body.

The fat man exited the room onto the landing where the thin man was waiting. The thin man did not hold out an olive branch; instead he gently placed his daughter into the open arms of the fat man and smiled. 'She looks like her mother.'

The fat man stepped back, wide eyed, like a frightened horse, and felt sure he would drop this small bundle of poison. And then he looked down upon the child. Her dark eyes sparkled up at him knowingly, and he saw his friend and his wife. 'No, she looks like you,' he said, his breath ragged. And he knew that despite his anger he would always love this child and his dear friend. It was what his wife would have done, and he would do anything for her.

Fished Off

by Kim Miller

The outboard started and Mark's boat pulled away, shore, sky and water touched by first light. The three of them, Mark, Stuart and Gav, promises of early nights kept, were escaping their hot, noisy working lives in the foundry by going fishing. Mark steered towards open water and took in a big breath, eyes closed.

This was his favourite time on the water: sunrise. He loved to hear the awakening land when he wasn't on it. Staccato dog barks, a lone cockerel shouting open the eyes of the day, birds singing and dotting the air over land and sea after some breakfast. The big sky's changing colours stretched out, moving on to other waters, other lands. Mark had a small thrill of devilment as though he shouldn't be there.

The contours of the coast, shapes and inlets, stood out sharply, ordnance survey writ large, then merged to a straight line, the edge of a solid mass, as the small boat's stab at a plucky roar took them further out. Mark gave the motor a pat of congratulation, followed by one for the boat – small, wooden, his pride and delight. An early purchase when he started at the foundry 20-odd years ago, it had been his faithful companion of escape.

'What you got in your sandwiches, Mark?' asked Stuart.

'Bloody hell, Stu. We've only been out here five minutes,' answered Mark, amused and quickly exasperated.

'It's been longer than that, and anyway, I was only asking. Didn't say I was going to eat them yet.'

Gav licked along the edge of a cigarette paper, wrapping it around the tobacco and sealing it with an air of approval. 'What do you want to know for?' he asked.

'We might have wanted to swap,' answered Stuart.

'We'll do sandwiches in a bit. Let's get further out first,' said Mark.

They hunched their shoulders, facing into early morning air that still held some pre-dawn steely pins.

To the east, the coastal town of Whitstable was also waking up, losing its stuttering night-time sparkle as lights went off. They could see the imposing elegance of the wind farm: vast, white, pointed sails turning with lofty idleness, chilly North Sea lapping their shins.

'Remember when we were on that charter out of Ramsgate and I was seasick?' asked Mark.

'Ooh, yeah, you were rough that day. You would go out with a hangover,' chuckled Gav.

'OK, thanks Mum,' said Mark.

Stuart laughed. 'Do you remember that bloke old Dave brought with him that day, standing over Mark with the bait bucket? Scooping handfuls out and letting them drop back in.' Stuart did a gruesome mime.

'Certainly do.' Gav leaned back, laughing.

'Don't. He was an animal. There I am, lying on a pile of stinking nets, begging for one of those out of body experiences you hear about, and he stands over me and eats a lug worm! Actually eats it! I *crawled* to the side of that boat, the bastard. Never been so ill in all my life.' Gav and Stuart were helpless, clutching bellies and slapping legs. 'Shut up you two.'

'State of him,' wheezed Stuart. 'Everyone's laughing, he's all floppy and green, eyes watering.'

'Bloody hell, don't,' pleaded Gav, exhausted.

'No, don't,' chuckled Mark, knowing it was funny really. He slowed the boat. 'This'll do us, plenty of gulls about. They must be after something.'

The engine was off, the anchor was dropped and rods were organised. A Thames Barge was making its way towards them heading seawards along the estuary.

'They're out early,' Mark thought, turning away to check the bait.

The water was ruffled by a mere finger-tip breeze, and the boat was steady. All three were jerked away from staring as a fish shot out of the water near the boat.

'Nearly gave me an 'eart attack,' said Gav, patting his chest in a mock fast heartbeat. 'Least we know there's fish out there.'

'Yeah, as long as the bastards start biting. Come on little fishies. Come and eat the lovely worms,' wheedled Stuart. 'Anyway, never mind them, what about these bloody sarnies?'

They had a ritual of not revealing the contents of their boxes until they were ready to eat. Small diversions were essential on the deadly days of no bites, terrible weather and frayed humours.

The others indulged him and grabbed their lunches, as they were passed by the smoothly sailing barge.

'Corned beef and tomato rolls,' announced Stuart.

Mark examined the cheese and pickle he had made last night and sank his teeth into a cut edge. Yesterday's bloomer was still pretty decent.

'BLT,' said Gav.

'Ooooh,' sing-songed Mark. 'Someone had their sandwiches made for them!'

'Hope they've gone soggy,' said Stuart with mock bitterness.

Gav bit off a large corner and waggled the remains at him. 'Cheers, mate.'

They stopped talking whilst they ate the agreed half of their lunches and fished drinks out of their bags. Stuart looked approvingly at a surprise pork pie he found.

Mark chewed and watched the barge move away from them. Enormous, rust-coloured sails dwarfed the low, liquorice torpedo barge they propelled. It slipped across the water like a curling stone on ice. Solid and gentle, dependable. It seemed to drag some of Mark's daily frustration behind it; a slow, uninvited water skier.

'Everything all right?' asked Stuart.

'Yeah, yeah, just my mum and dad, work, kids, all the usual. It'll be OK.'

'Right. No. I meant with the lines. We're not getting anything.'

Mark couldn't be bothered to move. 'Give it a bit longer.'

Gav reached over to one of the rods. 'Hold on, we've got something!'

Stuart jumped up. His excited foot caught the rim of the bait bucket and tipped it over.

'Oh, shit!' he yelled, as worms spread over the bottom of the boat. He lost his balance, tripping on the rattling bucket, and stumbled and skidded about in the small space, ending on his knees. Mark had to grab the side of the boat and lean right out over the water.

'Mind out!' he shouted.

'Fucking shut up, you two.' Gav's voice was raised too, mad with excitement.

The line pinged slack and there was instant disappointment. Gav pulled it in and dangled a small, tangled lump of stringy old net and empty mussel shells.

'Christ, it wasn't even a bite,' said Mark looking first at the old net and then at the mess in the boat. 'There's bloody worms everywhere.'

'Cor, thought I was going over then.' A relieved Stuart fanned his face with his hand.

'Would have served you right, you clumsy bastard,' grumbled Gav.

'It's not my fault you didn't have a bite.'

They looked at each other in the tiny space. Worms were everywhere and the gooey remains of several of them were smeared over Stuart's legs. They started laughing again, pointing at the wormy pool.

They scooped worms back into buckets as best they could

and sat down. Gav turned round to look further out to sea, his hand resting on the edge of the boat behind him.

'Aargh!' He yelled, 'what the... ?' He whipped round to inspect the back of his hand, the site of sudden pain. He pointed at the fish hook embedded in his skin. 'Who did that?' He was shocked and enraged.

'Idiot,' said Mark to Stuart, who guiltily dropped a rod.

'Cor! It was an accident.'

'I should hope it bloody was, an accident makes you an idiot; on purpose would make you a maniac.'

'These things happen,' Stuart claimed.

Gav wasn't sure he was getting his due as an injured party and voiced his feelings.

'They happen to you. You. More than anyone else, because you're a careless arsehole. And you still couldn't care less now! Arsehole.' Pale and shaking, he held his injured hand in the other. 'Have you got cutters?'

'Here,' said Mark. 'Never leave home without them. This is hardly a first, is it?'

'It was him then as well,' accused Gav.

'OK, let's get it sorted.' Mark pushed the embedded hook further through until it formed a pyramid of skin with a dark point of metal visible at its peak and then the barb broke through the surface. Gav gasped and jiggled his legs throughout.

'Baby,' snorted Stuart.

'We'll see how you like it in a minute.' Gav held his breath as Mark applied the cutters and snapped the teeth through the hook. He pushed the blunt end back the way it came and out of the skin. Gav sucked his freed hand and inspected it again, looking at Stuart in disgust. 'Cheers for that, Mark.' He pulled a face at Stuart, who stuck up two fingers at him – half cheery, half serious.

One of the lines twitched. Mark stopped his breath, leaned across with quiet expectation, and picked up the rod. He pulled on it and met with pleasing weight and solid resistance.

The others watched, poised.

'I think we might have something here.' His throat was tight; he held back his excitement to concentrate. He put more pressure on the line and felt a kick through the rod as the fish twisted and tried to pull away.

'Feels like a big old boy.'

'Come on Mark, bring the bugger in,' said wide-eyed Stuart.

'Bass, I reckon,' gabbled Gav.

The fish bolted away, taking a couple of yards of line with it. Mark countered hard and got a jolt as the fish stopped dead in its tracks, not strong enough. He steadied himself and the line against the resistance of the creature out of sight fighting for its life.

A few minutes' persistent pressure wore down the fish and Mark began to bring it in towards the boat. The others leaned round him, dying to see the fish as it came out of the water.

'It's big, get the net. Come on!' Mark was tense now, scared of losing at the last. The fish came clear of the water, still thrashing but helpless now. Gav leaned across with the net and took the weight from the line.

He put the net in the bottom of the boat and they pulled back its ropey folds, finding a large, twitching bass. Mark picked it up, held it against his body with one hand and took hold of the hook with the other. It had gone through cleanly and came out easily.

'That's a specimen, alright,' said Stuart, impressed. They nodded respectfully. 'Reckon that's six pounds.'

'Oh, *easy*,' joined in Gav.

Mark had a firm hold on the impressive fish; the scales ranged silver-white to black, muscular movement dotting them with tiny rainbows. He was scornful about the claimed six pounds.

'It's not as much as that, is it? Not six pounds.' The other two pulled faces and peered at it. 'It's a decent size though,' he relented.

'We'll be lucky to get any more like that today, in any case,'

Gav pointed out.

'True enough, who's gonna have it?' asked Stuart, wondering how to make a good case for himself.

'Dunno, see what else we get,' answered Mark. They checked the bait on all the lines and settled back down to wait. Stuart's head nodded dozily.

'What the fuck's that?' asked Gav, pointing.

A black shape floated about twenty yards from the boat.

'It's a slick or something.' Stuart gave it a cursory glance.

'Give over. Look, it's a big, 3D thing.' He made circular movements with his arms.

'Yeah, it does look like it,' Mark agreed, but sceptically.

Gav fought his corner. 'It is. Definitely. Look.'

They shifted around in the boat to get a proper look. It did seem to have bulk, although they knew the surface of the water could be deceptive, casting shadow, reflecting light. They stared hard.

'Could be a seal,' offered Mark.

'Could be.' Stuart nodded sagely.

'I reckon it's a body,' asserted Gav, quite excited.

'Yes, the body of a seal.' Mark's speech was deliberate and sarcastically patient.

'No, a real body, a person.'

Stuart rolled his eyes. 'Yet another drama.'

Gav pounced on the accusation. 'Oh, am I not supposed to mind? Good old Gav, feel free to plant lumps of poxy metal in him, draw blood if you like, he won't say a word.'

'It was a bloody accident!'

'It was acting like an idiot.'

Never mind, you two,' Mark intervened.

Gav tutted and rolled a cigarette. 'It's nearer now,' he said, lighting up. 'Have a look at it.'

'Why is it always me?' Mark grumbled.

'Cos it's your boat.'

Mark strained to get a better look. It was a dark, solid shape, Gav was right about that, and it appeared very bloated. Pretty horrible, whatever.

'It's a seal,' he said, confidently.

Stuart had an idea. 'Poke it with an oar.'

'Sod that. It's not near enough anyway.'

'It will be in a bit.'

'What's the point? It's definitely dead.'

'Just to see.'

They sat and watched it dipping and rocking in the small swells. 'It's near enough now,' Stuart gleefully announced.

'You do it.'

'It's your boat; go on.'

Mark picked up the oar, licking his lips made dry from sun and salt or nerves, and steeled himself. He got a good grip on the oar, leaned out and gave the mass a sound prod at the nearest end, sinking it a few inches and making the other end bob out of the water.

'What was that?' Gav was startled.

'Dunno, don't like it though.' Mark cringed, holding the oar in front of him.

'Do it again.'

'You do it.'

'Not all this again, just do it.'

Mark prodded again. The same thing; this time they were ready to have a good look.

'It looks like a head. It's definitely a body.' Gav was panicky.

Mark swallowed. 'It can't be, what would be the chances of that?'

'Never mind the sodding odds, just turn it over!' Gav was urgent, but glad to make someone else responsible. Stuart echoed his sentiments.

Mark puffed out his cheeks, remoistened his lips, took a breath and got the oar under the object. He flipped it. The oar skewed away. They groaned. He adjusted his position and ... flipped. The bulk slowly turned, looked like it would stop, then lurched and bobbed, face upwards.

What they called a face was a bloated mess, half eaten or

smashed off by a boat; unless it had happened on land. Bits of soft tissue, sodden and swollen, floated on the surface like grisly petals around a festering stamen. The body drifted away from them in the fading wake of a distant boat.

'Oh, Christ.' Mark was stunned, barely aware he had spoken.

Silence hung in the boat, hands went over mouths, then came dry retching and horrified groans.

'What shall we do?' asked Stuart.

'Told you it was a body,' crowed Gav, trying to regain some control and kudos.

'Well, you were bound to be right sometime,' sneered Stuart. 'Just cos you thought ...'

'Just shut up you two! Who cares? What are we going to do about that?' He pointed at the inanimate, putrid lump. 'Poor bloke,' he added, remembering what they were dealing with and accepting that it was human, as he thankfully watched it float further away.

'Phone the Coastguard.' Stuart waved his mobile around. 'I've got a signal.'

'Brilliant!' Mark pointed frantically at the phone. 'Do it, do it.'

He dialled. They waited. 'Coastguard please.' The others sighed with relief; they weren't on their own any more.

'What do you reckon happened?' wondered Mark.

'No idea, mate, no idea.' Gav shook his head slowly.

'Do you think that happened to his face in the sea or was he dumped like that?'

'No idea, mate.'

Sitting in sight of the corpse was unsettling and gruesome; the time passed slowly and they were fidgety and snappy.

'How much longer?' whined Gav.

'Oh, for God's sake, stop asking.' Stuart showed no under-standing despite feeling the same way. 'That might be them.' He pointed to a frothy dot in the distance lengthening to a trail as it neared. 'Yeah, that's definitely them.'

Stuart stood up excitedly, rocking the boat violently. Gav

lurched and clung to the side. An oar was dislodged; Mark lunged to keep it secure, slipped in the worm slime and went over into the water.

'Mark! Oh, shit, oh, Jesus! Get him, Stu, for fuck's sake, get him!'

Mark came to the surface taking rasping gulps of air. He looked frantically around, disorientated and desperate to get his bearings. He saw the boat, then, panicking, twisted and writhed in the water until he spotted the body. He swam, madly, the few strokes to the boat and grabbed the side.

'I don't wanna touch it, get me out. Get me out! Quick! I don't want that bastard thing near me!' he shrieked.

Stuart and Gav easily hauled him into the boat.

'That's disgusting.' Mark shivered with cold and revulsion.

'That was you again, you idiot,' Gav accused Stuart.

Stuart was aghast. 'How was it me?'

'Leaping around, of course.'

'They're nearly here,' interrupted Mark, watching the powerful dinghy skimming closer.

'You all right, lads?' called out one of the crew.

'Fine,' they called and waved in answer.

The coastguard manoeuvred the boat alongside the body and switched off the engine. Morbid fascination made the lads watch. After a short consultation amongst the crew of the big dinghy they restarted the engine and edged away.

'What you doing?' shouted Stuart.

The coastguards looked at him, deadpan. 'It's a seal, mate,' one of them said. They eased in the direction of the coast, then noisily increased speed away from the little boat.

'Whoops!' said Gav.

Stuart looked shame-faced. 'Anyone could have made that mistake.'

'Is there a drink anywhere?' Gav's mouth was stale and claggy from chain smoking.

Mark didn't speak. He started the boat and braced himself to freeze as they gained momentum across the water.

'We're not going home, surely?' Stuart was lavishly disbelieving. 'We were having such a lovely day.'

'Oh, yeah, nice and relaxing,' spluttered Mark, starting to grin.

'Like a holiday – I'm a new man!' Gav declared.

Mark looked to the coast then back at the boat: chaos, filth and two bickering idiots. Life on land seemed a bit easier now. He looked forward to getting home. He wouldn't even mind being sworn at by his wife, and told to get his manky gear off outside. Not sexy after a day in chest-high rubber, apparently.

He had a thought. 'And don't either of you even think about having that fish.'

'What?' they said.

'It's my boat, remember.'

Anniversary Tower

by Nick Hayes

The little boy sits in the shade of the breakwater looking out to the sea. All around him there is noise and there are people. His mother attends to his sister who has somehow got sand in her bright pink pants. His friends and their parents sit around on the pebbles and drink in the rays of summer. This is a balmy time.

The building of the grotters had always been a joyous point on the calendar. Each year his family had taken off on the bus into town with a rucksack full of drink and nibbles and a plan to build the Best Tower Ever. Each year they were somehow defeated by the incessant nagging of alcohol as the parents' engineering grew more and more haphazard. Or else in the twilight hours the children succumbed to fatigue and the grotters turned to so many shells amongst the wilderness of stones.

The boy sits in the shade and looks over to his mother and his sister and the gap. There is a hollow next to his mother and a space on the blanket. He has not yet grown accustomed to the gap although his mother thinks his silences are growing less deep and his eyes less dark over the last few months. He closes his eyes to the family fun and aches. His thoughts reach inside himself. He touches his emptiness and cannot find the bottom of it.

The grotters had once marked the start of a long, summer

of adventure. Trips on camping safaris to catch frogs and hunt snakes through long grass. Train treks to the city and West End shows bursting with colour and movement. Footballs kicked endlessly between each other as the sun ducks behind the Big Tree. Cricket bats and balls knocked up and over, far and near, wide and long, here and beyond. Those times were not here. The grotters marked the anniversary of the hospital visit. Barely any time had passed since four became three.

The boy edges out into the evening sun and places his hands into the colourful bucket of oyster shells. He lets them fall through his hands and the sound of their gentle chink nips at his memory. He takes out a handful and scatters them before him. His mother makes out she is not looking but smiles to herself and tells herself that everything will be all right. The shells are strangely chaotic and the opposite of uniform. He places them in a circle as the makeshift base and runs his finger over their greying surface.

Around him, some of the other families have built oyster shell palaces. The best effort – only yards away – reaches out grandly from the pebbles and narrows at the zenith like some seaside Shard. Seagulls swoop sheepishly away from the point to avoid its epic grandeur. Elsewhere, all the others he can see are taking shape – oyster shell cones with glorious decorations from yellow flowers and thin, wispy ribbons to beer cans and bottle tops.

The boy gathers up his puny base and drops the shells back into the bucket. He sighs and chews on the side of his mouth. Maybe he can close his eyes and travel back? He screws up his eyes but his sister's wailing drifts across the beach. She runs to him and throws herself around his neck.

'Big brother!' she exclaims in her baby voice. 'Big Brother Build Tower!' With that she dumps the oyster bucket upside down and runs off to a gaggle of children excitedly prodding at a washed up cod carcass.

He puts aside his thoughts and starts. He takes the shells one by one and the layers grow and the shape takes on some strength. Today he will build a grotter.

Magically, the grotter grows up into the air more impressive and more solid than any standing near. Almost in a moment it starts to dwarf all others on the beach. The boy soon stands on tip toes to place shells at the very top. He builds it with an abandon and a relish and a frenzy that starts to worry his mother and those around him. He starts to run to the stock pile for more oyster shells and bounds along the beach with buckets in both hands, bashing into bodies without care. His constructive vigour does not falter and his mother's words hold no sway as the dusk slips across the shore.

Without the stature to increase the height, he adds on layer after layer around the perimeter until the tower squats on the beach like an ominous oyster shell volcano. His hands now sore and marked, and his mother gathering up their things, he sits to gaze at his creation.

'It's for him,' he wheezes.

His mother smiles and nods. 'He would love it, darling.' She gently approaches him to pull him away and drape a warming layer around his shoulders. He shuffles uncomfortably but doesn't resist.

'Let's light it then,' he demands.

The beach is now a splendid shimmering dreamscape. Grotters sit proudly all across the beach. Their delicate tea lights shine brightly and smiling faces peer into them glowing gold.

Her son sits calmly in admiration of his tribute. The mother retreats to her friends' embrace and quietly cries. Her friends whisper to her words of comfort.

The boy gazes through the gaps of the grotter at the flickering flame beneath. There is a strange sense of calm and the coolness of the oncoming night time soothes him.

The sounds of the beach begin to fade from his ears and he hears only the rasping of his own breath. He looks at his creation with pride. His eyes run around the contours of the tower. He takes in each layer and every creamy shell. The light jumps a little in a hint of breeze.

He thinks he sees a face in the shadows. A face in the heart of his grotter. His body tenses and he leans forward. He looks closer and the features emerge from the blackness. His breath has stopped. All he can do is look and wonder. He sees him there in the night. He feels a wave of warmth engulf him and his eyes fill with tears.

As he blinks them away he realises the tears bring the face into focus. Through the swell of teardrops he can see the eyes, the nose, the mouth. He can see him smiling at him. He can almost touch him. He stifles an animal sob so he can listen.

The mouth moves. The words come.

'I love you, son.'

Private View

by Laura Sehjal

Everyone's stood around with half-full, luke-warm glasses of wine in hand. Chatting. I look down, shuffle my feet, then realise that I can see a lot of brogues: brown, black, brown and white, black and white. I realise, with an accepting sniff, that my carefully picked converse look shabby despite the dinner jacket I'm wearing over my T-shirt. I always manage to misjudge this type of event.

I wonder what everyone is saying. Perhaps it's better not to know. I can feel my chest getting a little tighter, my neck feels a little redder.

A big-named curator is across the room from me. He still has his sunglasses on. Sunglasses would have been a good idea; the fact that it's evening time, indoors and dimly lit would have bothered me a little, but at least part of my face would have been covered. They say that you can tell the most about what a person is thinking or feeling from their eyes, don't they? I'd really like my eyes to be covered right now.

'Great exhibition Jeff!' I turn sharply to see my friend Simone, in light tanned brogues and a black mac that she hasn't taken off yet... I doubt that she will take it off; it must be part of her outfit. Relief floods over me as she leans in to kiss my cheek. As I pull back I realise, too late, that she is going in to kiss my other cheek and I leave her hanging mid-air, lips puckered. I attempt a chortle and shuffle my converse some more. Then I realise that I'm drawing attention to them and stop.

Simone slips a graceful arm through my awkward one and begins to guide me around the room. I sigh and muscles relax that I didn't even know were tense. I only invited her because she has recently split up with her boyfriend; I thought the Private View might distract her.

'So,' she says, 'Your work is obviously the best here. Everyone is talking about it and I've caught wind of the words "solo-show" being banded around in relation to your name, darling!'

When Simone says the word 'darling', she does so with a mocking drawl that makes me feel even more at ease. I stare gratefully into her pale blue eyes and am just about to ask her who might be banding around the term 'solo-show', when my old friend Dan squeezes my shoulder. I turn. He is also in converse, but then he's new in town. I make introductions, badly, and then look around the room. I lift my wine to my mouth and bite the glass a bit. Simone and Dan look at each other, realise that they must both know me quite well when the other one looks apologetic, and laugh.

I'm being asked questions about the relation of theme to material in my current work. I look urgently around the room for Simone, I only invited her because she broke up with her boyfriend, but it would be really good if she were here right now. I try to disengage. It doesn't work. The questions have moved on to who has influenced my current work. I come to the conclusion that the interrogator thinks that I've ripped off another artist rather than create an original sculpture, and I try to justify myself, whilst looking for Simone. I spot her and Dan still talking in front of an abstract painting. Good. Both still here.

An introduction is made to the big-named curator. I shake his hand and worry I was rather limp-wristed. He is talking to me about his opinion on last month's 'Art Review', when I notice Simone touch Dan's shoulder. My breathing stops: just a brush, that's all, a gesture, a way of saying, 'we're going to be friends'. I breathe again.

My opinion is asked for. I agree with the guy in the brogues, only I try to add a hint of cynicism. Everyone is laughing. Dan has his hand on Simone's hip and is whispering in her ear. They have gotten much closer. I try to find a way to end the conversation, but more people have entered the circle and are comparing my work to someone who recently had a show at the Serpentine Gallery.

I feel bile in my throat and am confused as to why it is there. I feel the pressure of having to say the right thing and wish that Simone's arm were still in mine. It isn't; it is on Dan's arm as he carries on whispering in her ear, near the abstract painting.

As the sunglasses-wearing, big-named curator asks if I am interested in having a solo exhibition, I notice Dan's hand move to the small of Simone's back. I am asked if I have a body of work yet, and do I have any other exhibitions under my belt. Simone turns to catch my eye, moves as if to come and speak to me, my heart rate picks up, she sees who I'm talking to, holds up her hand in an, 'I'll-leave-you-to-it gesture', whilst shaking her head to let me know that what she was about to say isn't important.

I want to hear what she was going to say. I'm sure it *was* important. I'm setting up a meeting for Wednesday this week. I'm asked if I like the 'White Box' gallery, I'm saying 'yes' and Dan is guiding Simone out of the building, his hand slipping dangerously near her bum. Simone is giggling as they slip through the warehouse doors.

I stare dumbfound at the curator, who is shaking my hand and congratulating me on the next step in my career. 'Next time, you'll be solo,' he says. My heart sinks.

Half Life

by Joanne Bartley

I recognised the machine's ticking from my science lessons at school. Radiation was everywhere. My teacher had even pointed a Geiger counter at a banana and the dial had moved. I tried to feel reassured, but I knew Callum had brought danger to our house.

Half life was a half-remembered concept from my school days, but didn't it mean radiation lessened over time? Atomic particles fizzed with life, then fizzed half as much, and half again as their power weakened. I could only hope the ticking from the cupboard under the stairs would fade away.

Callum had found us this bungalow on a street between a council estate and a road of millionaires' houses. The rent was cheap because the landlord had a drug problem and couldn't care less. I scrubbed the black mould away every few days. I fought a battle with the cooker he refused to repair. I didn't think of this as home. I walked down Joy Lane to get to the shops. I decided joy was achieved with cash and a life lacking chaos.

When I cried Callum only shouted, 'I got you the fucking sea!'

I knew Callum wanted a grand gesture. He'd ripped my life to shreds but that wasn't enough. He wanted to destroy on a bigger scale. He kept guns in his den. I knew the theme of his thoughts. Why not pick on a posh little town by the sea?

Why not pick on tourists and smug Londoners buying houses bigger than they could afford in the capital? Why not pick on ordinary people who had done nothing wrong, because what had they done right either?

My man, the evil supervillain.

Not really. He was all about gestures and posing. He would never actually go through with this.

I found the device in the cupboard under the stairs when Josh lost his PE kit. The PE bag would never be there, but I'd looked everywhere else. I was yelling, 'Do you know how much those fucking trainers cost?'

The evidence of Callum's evil silenced me. The cupboard was full of wires and canisters, and boxes and sellotape. Yes, sellotape. The destructive plan that had fascinated him for months could be as ordinary as finding an edge on a roll of tape. This dangerous hobby he read about online led him to build a homemade contraption as amateur as Josh's school projects. I could have laughed, it was all such madness… But I shut the door quickly, my breathing too fast.

'Just get out!' Josh grabbed his coat. 'Just get to school!'

I imagined a Hiroshima cloud above Wheeler's Oyster Bar. I imagined beach huts exploding in a nuclear glow. Then as the hours passed I returned to worrying about real life. Would Josh get a detention for having no PE kit? Could we afford new trainers and shorts? The nuclear bomb in the cupboard was less real than having no food and the oven playing up again.

I hated life. Hated it. I trudged to the shops for eggs as I always did. I bought Callum the cheapest beer.

I knocked on his den door because he didn't like me going in unannounced. I sewed a pair of jeans that didn't fit me any more. I cleaned the mould. Josh came home from school and I yelled at him for leaving his clothes on his floor. I hated him for making me pick them up. I hated the washing machine with its cracked knob that wouldn't turn. It was as bad as the cooker. I could call the landlord, or send Josh to school with a ketchup stain on his uniform.

Next day I held a pan scrubber under the tap. 'Come here.' I soaked the stain.

'I'm getting wet!'

Water dripped from Josh's jumper to the kitchen floor. I doubted it would dry on the ten minute walk to school.

Callum's weed was under our bed. I would take some when he went out to sign on, it could be my treat.

'My teacher said I should take a test.'

I couldn't do Josh's homework; a test would only mean more trouble. 'What test?'

'If I pass I go to grammar school. There's a letter in my bag.'

'Grammar school? Are we living in the nineteen fifties?'

'It's called the Kent Test. If you pass it means you go to a better school.'

He got a letter out of his school bag. I skim read it and noted all the blank boxes to fill in.

'Simon's brother goes, there's a chess club at his school and he won a prize. I'd like to learn chess.'

He was looking at me. I hated to see the hope in his eyes. I would screw the letter up, throw it in the bin and pour his wet rice krispies on top of it.

Water dribbled down his wrecked jumper. What would Josh do in a grammar school? I held the paper in my hand. Too many boxes.

I heard Callum moving upstairs. Would I dare to steal my smoking treat?

'I was supposed to give it to school yesterday but I forgot. I don't know what to do.'

I thought of the nuclear threat in our under stairs cupboard. I thought of the big houses on Joy Lane and the joy of the families who lived inside them. I remembered the first time Josh had written 'mum' on a crayon picture. I remembered when he was Joseph in the school nativity play. I felt so proud. Why not hope? Why shouldn't my boy go to a grammar school?

I grabbed a pen and scrawled my name in the signature box.

Let the school do the rest.

'Take the test, get yourself in to grammar school and buy yourself a millionaire mansion.'

'Right, Mum, that's the plan!' He had that cheeky confidence sometimes, it always pissed Callum off.

He was dabbing his jumper with a kitchen towel. He dropped it and snatched the paper out of my hand. 'I'll fill in all the rest of it.'

'Whatever. You'll be late for school. It'll dry.'

Callum's footsteps on the stairs.

'Okay, I'm going!'

I picked the kitchen towel off the floor. Why was it me that always did everything? Life was shit. I'd thought this many times before. But today was signing-on day and after my mould scrubbing I'd steal a treat. Today was almost a holiday.

Callum looked hung over. 'Did you get bacon?'

I couldn't afford bacon. I shook my head. 'I'll get you some later.'

He sat down and I went to fetch his coffee. I got away with no bacon; maybe it was a good day after all.

'Josh is going to try to get to grammar school.'

'Grammar school, what the fuck?'

'They have some test.'

'What test? He's ten years old and thick as shit.'

'There was a letter from the school.'

Why had I signed that? The big house on Joy Lane might as well be on the moon.

Callum's ever-present anger had a new theme. 'Grammar school! It's like Downton Abbey in tory shithole Kent. They just want to keep us in our place.'

I would tell Josh not to mention the test again.

'Have you got any money?'

'A fiver maybe.' I'd have nothing left if I gave that to him.

I passed the under stairs cupboard as I went to get my purse. I wanted a massive explosion to tear Callum's angry head from his ugly body. I wanted a mushroom cloud to engulf our whole town with its poncy harbour, fake-as-shit castle and rotten pebbly beach. I wanted it destroyed in a massive thermonuclear fireball. I wanted to explode into a million pieces too.

Then I thought of Josh, taking his test. I wanted him to go to grammar school and to university. I wanted him to live on Joy Lane.

I found £7 in my purse. I hoped it would be enough to make Callum happy. I hoped he'd forget about bacon. I hoped I could find something to feed everyone. I hoped the hob would work. I hoped in my planned fug of weed smoking that I could be bothered to cook.

Hope was weird. I hoped life would hurt less. I hoped Josh would pass a test and blast off in his escape pod to a better world.

On his birthday we'd stuck glow-in-the-dark stars on his bedroom ceiling. I asked him to make a wish. He didn't tell me what he wished for. I don't know if he even made a wish or not. He asked me if the stars were radioactive. There was a Geiger counter in the downstairs cupboard but I didn't check. I supposed he'd learned about radiation at school.

Callum used to work at Dungeness. He hated the job but we had money and an easier life back then. Money had brought problems too. His obsession began. He bought every book on Armageddon he could find. He bought a lock for his den door. He bought guns. I don't know where he got them from.

He closed web pages if I went near his laptop, but I knew what he was doing. He wanted to be bigger than he was. He didn't just want to make a mark, he didn't have a clue how to make a mark… No, he wanted to blow a fucking great big hole in the world. He was hatching a plan to destroy everything. What a hobby.

I supposed I could have thought to stop him, but taking control was never my style. Maybe I did nothing because the idea dazzled me too? To blow a hole where a shithole town had once been, that was crazy and also awesome. Sparkling into a million pieces in a gigantic explosion… some days that thought appealed. An explosion ended all the shit.

None of it was real anyway. It was hard enough to deal with day to day stuff. A broken cooker made me cry, how could I deal with the nuclear bomb under the stairs? It was easy to ignore.

The lady on the till at the Co Op was friendly. Josh chatted about a new school reading book. Life had its good bits sometimes. Callum was engrossed in his hobby and mostly left me alone. He used to build Airfix models of bombers, but that didn't mean he'd ever fly a war plane. Perhaps one day he'd simply dismantle the bomb and move on to train spotting or darts.

'It's the Kent Test today.'

'What test?' Callum asked.

'The grammar school test.'

Why did the idiot kid not listen? I'd told him not to mention the test.

'You don't need a test for a fucking grammar school.'

'Why not? Lots of my friends are doing it.'

'It's not for us. What would you do in a school like that?'

'I don't think I'll get in.'

'Of course you won't. So don't try. Do you know how much the uniforms cost? They wear blazers and shit.'

'I signed the letter, he'll be on the list to do it now.' I hoped Callum wouldn't make me ring the school.

'Stupid shit. Stupid!'

I didn't know if Callum was referring to the test, or Kent schools, or Josh, but the moment passed. He finished his coffee and went to get the post.

I helped Josh find his coat and kissed him. 'Good luck,' I whispered to him.

'Thanks, I'll do my best.'

'Don't worry, we'll sort everything if you pass,' I told him.

'We'll see.' Josh grabbed his bag and left.

Callum had ripped an envelope open and was staring at a letter with venom. 'What the…!'

I approached Callum with caution.

'What is it? What does the letter say?'

'The bastard wants us out. He's selling the house.'

'The landlord?'

'Of course the fucking landlord.'

'We can find somewhere else, don't worry.'

'We can't. One month, he wants us out by fucking October the sixteenth!'

'That's not long.'

'It's impossible. We can't move.'

The under stairs cupboard with its wires and deadly fuel and sellotape. The homemade bomb didn't look portable. If it couldn't be transported could it simply be defused …?

'Fuck, fuck, fuck, fuck!' His anger was toxic.

I reached for my phone. 'I'll look at estate agents.' I could find a website, show him a cheap house up the road and make everything better.

My head hit the kitchen counter. I felt his breath hot on my neck. I saw my phone smash into the wall and shatter. His knee pressed in to my thigh with so much force I yelped. I closed my eyes so I could see nothing. I attempted to turn invisible in my mind. He wanted destruction and my silence always gave him less satisfaction. A shove next, but it barely hurt. He was gone. It didn't usually happen that way. Maybe the whole town would take his anger next? I tensed myself fearing destruction, but I waited and the world just continued.

Only me then. I didn't know whether to be glad.

The day passed in a blur, the phone screen was wrecked and I couldn't be bothered to sort it out. I picked up the pieces and put the lot in an envelope. Maybe it would be good if I played less app games.

I felt sorry for myself and watched TV until 3.37. That time was my happy time, my boy came home a minute or so either side. I loved my boy. My head was still throbbing from its encounter with the kitchen counter, my heart still ached, but I felt joy when I saw my ten year old with his Minecraft bag.

'Hi mum.' He looked happy. I was happy.

'How did the test go?' I asked.

'It was hard,' he said. 'I don't know. Maybe it'll be ok.'

'It'll be fine.'

I hoped so hard it hurt.

He went upstairs to plug himself into his Playstation. I wouldn't ask about his homework today. None of it mattered. None of it mattered. Ever.

A month of lying low followed. Neither of us looked at estate agents. Josh had no idea. The days were endured. If we spoke of moving out then it might become real.

Callum didn't let me out of his sight; we even went to the shops together. The nice lady at the Co Op said we must be very much in love. We got drunk, we got stoned, we got by. I worried, or didn't care, or wanted it all over, depending on my mood each day. Sometimes I thought I should try to stop him. Then when he looked at me I knew he was my life.

He kept his laptop in his den mostly, but one day I found it on our bed. The browser window was open at a picture of a blackened child. He was downstairs so I had my opportunity. I sat on the edge of the bed and opened a new browser window, pure white with a search box. This was my chance.

I typed, 'Kent Test pass dates.'

'The results for the Kent Test will be sent out on 15 October 2016.'

The end of things must be before October 16th and the test results were the day before. I didn't know his plan for the bomb, but every major thing in his life was left until the last minute. He'd even proposed on February 28th when he thought I might propose in the leap year. Of course we wouldn't ever get married, he didn't have a deadline.

When we walked to the Co Op the next day Callum seemed in a good mood. His benefit had been paid. The houses of Joy Lane looked even more appealing in the autumn sun. A woman with nice clothes pushed a buggy to a front door.

'Do you think Josh will ever live in a house like that?' I asked.

'A big house with a view of the sea?'

The mum smiled at her child. It was so normal but so different, both at the same time.

'No,' Callum said. 'The world will never be happy for us, they live in some smiling buy-anything world. The fuckers give us nothing, ever.'

I saw him eye the happy well-dressed mother and her small child. I saw his hate and I saw his decision made.

Hope was scatty, hope was indistinct. Maybe his plan wouldn't work. Maybe I was wrong and it wasn't a bomb at all. I used to hate PE. When I walked to school I imagined a bomb from Russia would come and PE wouldn't happen, or the teacher would get ill, or there'd be a fire. Maybe I was just an idiot with a wild imagination. He told me I was an idiot.

The calendar brought only bad news. October passed quickly if you willed the days to slow down.

'We need to be out of here tomorrow.' I dared to voice the truth.

It was as if he didn't hear the words. He was drinking, he'd been drinking since breakfast. Armageddon was to be fuelled by Co Op own brand lager.

I decided to repair my phone. I needed sellotape. The sellotape was in the under stairs cupboard.

Callum was distracted, he was looking at the weird stuff on his laptop.

The deadly device was a few pieces bigger than when I'd last looked. The Geiger counter was switched off but I didn't need to hear its ticking. Bombs ticked in films, didn't they? I needed no signal of impending doom. I grabbed the sellotape and ran to the bedroom.

I found the edge of the tape with shaking hands. My phone was my only link to the outside world. I took it out of the envelope and taped its pieces back together. The screen was cracked but when I switched it on its light shone.

I should call the police. I could reach out to someone…

But it was results day.

It was 3.37. I scanned my emails. Nothing from the council. Perhaps Josh had written my email address wrong. Perhaps Callum had got to Josh and he hadn't really taken the test.

I felt the prickle of radiation in the air. No one felt radiation. It must have been my imagination. I rubbed my arm, trying to feel something real. I checked my fine arm hairs to see if they stood on end. No, that was static electricity. How silly I was.

Radiation lost its power. Half life meant it was half its value. It decayed and it was half as bad again... But all that took thousands of years. It was never safe, not in any way that had meaning.

There was a half life to hope too. Josh had looked at the stars on his ceiling and said he would be an astronaut. He once told me he wanted to climb a mountain. He said when he grew up he would get a fast car. He changed as he got older, the stars came off his ceiling, the mountains didn't inspire him, he said he would get a car one day, just a decent car, it would be fast enough. Today depending on a test result his hope might take another hit.

I felt Callum's presence in the doorway and closed my eyes. He let me be and I sensed him move on. His head would be full of doubts too. Years ago he'd said he'd buy me a diamond ring. I'd once hoped we'd be a happy couple.

I hit refresh. The email appeared. 'Your Kent Test Results.'

I scanned the details. Josh's name, some dates and information... Then, 'Please be advised that your child has been assessed as suitable for a Kent high school.'

High school? I read the message again. No mention of the grammar school. I thought about the words. It made sense, it kind of made sense, high school not grammar school, but it wasn't quite clear. The spider cracks of my broken phone couldn't hide the truth. I accepted the worst, this meant no grammar school. This meant no bright future for my child. No university or shining career. No Joy Lane.

3.38. Josh would be home from school any moment and I would need to break the news to him. I would say it was fine. I would say grammar schools were overrated. I would say it was a silly dream, I would reassure him that it didn't mean he was stupid like Callum said. I would soothe his tears and convince him there was still hope.

He would cry and cry, because life was shit. Yes. Shit shit shit. Life was shit!

I went downstairs, I would be ready. Could I do this? I heard it… Not the door opening, the sound of sorrow.

Sobs forced through gasps for air. Tears flowing. Despair.

Standing by the door to the under stairs cupboard, Callum was sobbing like a child. His tears came fast, he shook, he disintegrated, he was a disappointed wreck of a man.

'I know, I know…' I held him. I understood.

'It's hopeless,' he said.

'It's shit,' I agreed. 'It's all shit.'

We sunk to the floor. Together we knew. His hand reached for the lever on the nuclear device. I grasped his hand. I pushed his hand towards the lever. Together, as one, we would end the pain.

Joy Lane would be gone.

The Flat

by RJ Dearden

It was the same fantasy every night. I would see myself taking my claw hammer to His pride, to His joy. It was the only way I could get to sleep. Long after midnight, I'd imagine myself scraping the sharp edge of the tool down the side of His panther black BMW, the metallic screech as beautiful as a violin concerto. Leaping onto the bonnet, I would jump like a demented child on a bouncy castle, the bonnet buckling under my weight. Finally, a berserk wrecking glee would possess me and I'd run amok, caving in the windows. By the time I got round to slashing the tyres, I'd be snoring like a baby. Damn near worked every time.

It was the incessant cocaine chatter from HIM – our beloved next door neighbour – that stopped Mary from sleeping as well. Call me selfish but I wasn't willing to share the soporific secret in case she derided the fantasy, robbing it of the magic. Anyway, Mary had other reasons to stay awake, she was always on the look-out for the little boy she'd seen that one night, standing over the bed. At the time, I'd laughed it off, saying she'd just woken up and projected whatever dream she was having out of her head. But I made damn certain she couldn't see my eyes when I said that. The Flat wasn't Scooby Doo spooky but the sense of a third person was always there. Worse thing, the presence seemed to like us.

Mary and I were what you might call 'blowthroughs',

tumbleweed working its way around the Kent coast. It's funny what being e-fitted in the local paper can do to a man. We spent a summer hiding out in a Dymchurch caravan living off the ill-gotten gains, or rather as we put it, the rewards of finders' keepers. Then, just as it started to get cold, an offer came to settee surf above the old Woolworths in Hythe. Then to a damp basement in Sandgate, afterwards a poky terrace in Folkestone. We try hard to forget the crazy house-share in Dover with the weirdo who kept hitting on Mary and the loft deal in Deal, well that's always been a blur. By the time we washed up in Whitstable, we were running on empty, exhausted by all the relocation, relocation, relocation. We hauled our possessions to the top floor, heaving the sofa and bed up the rickety stairs, and sighed. Enough was enough. No more running. It had only been five grand that we'd liberated from a misplaced suitcase on a train. Nobody was hunting us.

We burnt all our cardboard boxes on the beaches by Tankerton slopes in a drunken Viking ceremony during the baking hot summer of '01. It felt right and the Flat smiled benevolently down, rewarding us with some passionate years. Wonderful Whitstable. We used to buy hot croissants from the Parisian baker in the morning. He'd make lewd comments in French to Mary thinking I didn't understand but what the hell did I care? She got free cakes and chocolate croissants for just fluttering her eyelashes and I scoffed the tribute back in the Flat.

The insults in this town made me laugh. I remember the first time I got called a 'DFL' in Harbour Street. It was a badge of honour. 'Down from London' indeed! I began explaining our coastal odyssey to the paint stained local but his eyes glossed over.

'Whitstable Chic,' Mary called the local fashion sense, rolling her eyes. 'Why is everyone always decorating in this town?'

The Flat was on the third floor of a Victorian terrace. To say it was bizarrely shaped would be a kindness. The bedroom reminded me of a Toblerone bar cut down the middle – a steep sloping ceiling that I banged my head on a million times; so cold, you could see your breath in winter. A corridor took you to the lounge – long enough to play ten pin bowling on rainy Sundays. The lounge was spacious with sea views and overlooked the Castle. I had to pee with my knees bent due to another sloping ceiling in the loo. The whole place was like a fairground house of crazy angles. The acoustics were unpredictable too and it was hard to know where the other person actually was. Mary spilt hot tea on us as she turned from the kitchen and I stepped out of the loo. So we began calling out to each other like sailors in a sea fog, using echo to locate the other.

'Hello!'

'I'm in the lounge!'

'I'm turning the corner from the kitchen!'

'I'm leaving the bedroom!'

'I know … I'm right behind you.'

I suppose if I'm being honest, the downward spiral in the Flat started before He arrived in. To pinpoint the end of the good times, it was when Sarla and Mason moved in, two teenage junkies who sublet the damp basement flat. Late night chaos, missing mail … yeah, Sarla and Mason pissed all the tenants off. One guy even put a lock on the fire door to separate Them from Us. What about the smell of them? God, they stank, mostly of crap and BO. But funnily enough they didn't stop us sleeping. Not much. We could bolt the door from their chaos but there was no hiding from HIS incessant chatter.

'He lives to give people directions,' Mary announced one day. 'He's a much sought after geographical expert. A sage. Perhaps even an oracle. A human GPS.'

'Say what?' I said.

'Well look,' she said, pointing out the window. 'The car pulls up, our helpful neighbour rushes down, sticks his head in the window … hey presto, he's told them how to find their way. Off they go.' Car tyres screeched to prove her point.

'Erm, baby,' I said, 'he's selling. He's a dealer. You know …

drugs?'

'No shit, Sherlock,' she said, shaking her head. 'We could call the police …'

I arched an eyebrow.

Things improved slightly when he got a regular girlfriend and they would nod off after fifteen minutes of hurried love making. But before long it'd be back to same old same old.

'Yeah, yeah, yeah, yeah. Sniff. Sniff. Sniff. What? What? What?'

'We gotta get out of this place,' Mary whispered one night in the dark.

'Go where?' I said, half conscious, tossing the imaginary claw hammer from hand to hand. Maybe tonight I'd start with the headlights. What if I used a sledge-hammer? Would a rubber mallet be as fun? Did I even have a rubber mallet?

'Tell me your secret!' she demanded, jabbing me awake.

'I dunno,' I said. 'Shut your eyes and count to a thousand.'

'He was a little boy, you know,' she said. 'Six, maybe seven years old. Wearing a green jumper. Just watching us sleep. Watching you sleep. He had his arms folded. Holes in the elbows. Jet black hair. Pale skin. He was just staring at you,' she said. 'I even remember how his shoes were scuffed and the dullness of the buckles.'

Ah, the ghost. 'You were dreaming,' I muttered. 'Ghosts don't exist.' Mary had Fosbury Flopped back into bed the night she saw the boy, landing under the duvet behind me in one fluid movement. She'd broken the laws of geometry by not colliding into the steep ceiling.

'When do you think the little boy lived?' she asked. 'Poor little thing, I wondered what killed the little blighter. Do you think it's cold being dead?'

'There's no ghost, you imagined it,' I said.

'I've never been so sure of something in my life!'

I had a deep connection with Mary but I wished she stop wittering so I could imagine I was slashing HIS upholstery – I always forgot to do that. God, HE loved that Beemer, valeting it every Sunday on Tankerton Road. Wash, rinse, chammy, wax and shine. Even used a toothbrush on the alloys. This evening, my imaginary weapon would be a bowie knife. Blade slashing leather would be so comforting.

'Little boy drown,' I muttered, my voice floating from my subconscious mind. 'Tide got him. Playing on "The Street." Sinking sand ...'

'What?' She poked me. 'What did you just say? You always said I imagined it.'

I sat up rubbing my eyes. 'Dreaming, baby. Go back to sleep.'

'Christ, Paul! I can't bloody sleep!' she wailed.

Next door His monotone chatter paused then started again, inane words spilling from his mouth, idiocy compounded by foolishness. I yawned. 'You want me to beat the wall with the cricket bat again?'

She shrugged, dragging the duvet off the bed, leaving me cold, traipsing off to the lounge like a fatigued refugee. 'You can freeze for all I care. Selfish bastard.'

OK, it wasn't all bad. Did I mention we lived opposite the poet Neil Rogers? Great guy, real shame what happened to him. We once chatted whilst he extracted pigeons from the cavities from the walls of our building. Standing atop a ladder, he used the legs of the ladder to move left and right like a circus giant on stilts.

'You want me to hold the bottom of that, man?'

'Nah, be fine,' he said, yanking the ladder along, and tilting back until he pushed forward. My heart skipped a systemic beat. 'You ever leaving this place? You've been here forever.'

'It's cheap,' I said. 'We've got a ghost. He won't let us go.'

Mary gasped entering the lounge. 'What the hell is wrong with you?' she asked me. 'Go down and hold the bottom.'

Neil pulled a pigeon out, stroking it tenderly, the thing cooing back at him. The ladder started tilting back, a foot and a half from the roof. Finally he let the bird go, grabbed the guttering, laughing. 'You two look shattered.'

'Paul's fine,' she complained. 'He's got a little secret sleeping aid.'

We always got a great view of the carnival, our landlord dancing on a float as he waved jovially up at us every year. Nobody wore a Hawaiian shirt better than our landlord. And I shouldn't forget the fireworks. New Year. The Regatta. The Oyster Festival. Front row seats, every time. Sometimes, it felt like there were explosions every other night. But inexorably, like the volume dial on a record player, the misery was turned up little by little. The junkies in the basement flat got beaten within an inch of their lives one Sunday afternoon. Piercing screams and the police. On a Sunday afternoon! Neil had told us the walls of their flat were caked in blood. We flooded the second floor flat below us twice and got banned from using our shower until the plumbing was fixed. Captain Hawaii went silicone happy fixing the problem. That was a hot summer too – a sweaty one. Mary and I took turns washing in a gorilla tub, which we tipped down the only working plumbed outlet – the toilet. Before long it was winter again. Then there was the Christmas Day when HE begged for his life.

'I'll get you the money, I promise. I promise. I will,' our faceless tormentor begged.

'No second chances!' a gravelly voice replied.

'I will man, I will. Please don't shoot me. Please, man.'

The thought of bullets coming through the paper thin walls frightened the shit out of us. We had to get out of this place. We tried, I mean we tried. One place we looked around, the exiting tenant winked at me as I walked in. I spent the whole tour trying to work that wink out as the landlady gave us the ins and outs. It was only when we talked rent, deposits and bills that I got it … she was a money grabber, putting the rent up twice before we even got to sign. The Flat called us back.

The girlfriends He saw changed back and forth. Sometimes we saw them, posh blonde girls. He must have had something going for him. Different noises. Different chatter. Still, the only thing that kept me going was dreaming about the destruction of the precious car. My secret therapy. There was one Saturday morning, I left 'Reverend Black Grape' playing at top volume on a loop from 7 am to 12 pm to punish him and his pals after a particularly bad night when they had spouted torrents of nonsense at each other in a six-hour amphetamine frenzy.

We flooded the flat below again, my fault ... note to the world – tapioca should never be poured down the sink. More gorilla tub washing. An artist moved into the basement flat. Lovely fella, can't remember his name. Mary saw the little boy again. I lied some more. Most nights we spent tramping up and down the long corridor, duvet and pillows under arms, from bed to sofa and back again, seeking comfort, or silence; just sleep. We were refugees, cursed into an endless insomnia. Please just let us sleep. Still He kept talking. He couldn't stop. He fell asleep with the TV on. He yelled down the mobile. He snorted and snorted all night long. He argued with girls. He struck match after match burning box after box.

The claw hammer fantasy started involving his skull. We yelled, we screamed, we thumped the walls. He was impervious to it all. We had to get out of this place.

'Tell me your secret!' Mary demanded whenever I dozed off, poking me.

One day I walked to the end of 'The Street' at low tide and launched the claw hammer into the sea, throwing it as far as I could. The temptation to use the thing was strong. The hammer had begun serenading me from the toolbox, the sight of its curved head making me dizzy. I'd be hearing voices next.

I remember one of the posh blondes wailing up and down Tankerton Road on discovering she'd been replaced. Slamming doors. Tears in the street. Fists punching furniture. He took to head-butting the walls when he lost the plot.

One Saturday night at three am, I woke up, Mary's side was cold. She'd left the duvet behind so I guessed she hadn't decamped to the settee. I found her at the corridor intersection, between lounge and kitchen, jumping up and down, her arms flailing in the air.

'Babe, what you doing?'

'I've got to catch this moth.'

I couldn't see anything. 'It's just a moth?'

'I gotta catch it.'

As I lay back down, I decided tomorrow I would have a TALK with him. So what if He had mates? I didn't care about His 'connections.' We were going nuts. If I lost it, so what? We could go to Herne Bay. When a man buries his temper, one day he either kills himself or someone else. I knew which I'd prefer.

Mary slid back into bed, feet like icicles.

'Did you get the moth?' I asked.

'Problem fixed.'

'I dream about killing His car. Smashing it to pieces. It's the ultimate catharsis.'

'Hah!' she squealed with delight. 'Brilliant. Imagine if we both dreamt it? I'm going to start right away.'

The next second it was morning and I woke up naturally; refreshed; rested. I felt amazing. Mary stirred beside me. Something was different. Almost magical, like the silence of a snowy day. We fooled around a bit before getting up. I made fresh coffee for me and tea for her.

'Oh, my God!' A squeal of sheer delight came from the lounge. 'You won't believe this.'

I rushed in, seeing her standing with her back to me, the grey sea framing an excited silhouette. I saw what she was looking at and a pulse of pleasure raced through my veins. There HE was. Our night time tormentor. Outside. But He was sheepish now. Cowed. The precious car was a total write-off. The engine had been torched. The rest of the car was somehow in pristine condition. But there was no hiding the gaping burnt out hole where the engine had once been. I marvelled at the perfection of the job. Wow! You had to admire vandalism like that – not even in my wildest fantasies had I ever dreamt of that.

He spent the rest of the Sunday standing guard at the carcass of his former vehicle, His friends offering him solace and protection in numbers. He glowered up and down Tankerton Road, daring whoever had done it to step forward, a knuckle duster on his right fist. But He knew it; He'd been castrated.

'Do you think…?' Mary asked. 'I mean do you? That we, err …'

Inside, a sense of guilt grumbled in my belly like a dodgy kebab I had been too boozed-up to remember scoffing. Out of the corner of my eye, I glimpsed the little boy in a green jersey watching us, a smile curling up his bottom lips.

It wasn't long after that the Flat finally let us go.

Me and My Gull

by Alison Kenward

Well, that's just typical, isn't it? Standing right in my way. No intention of moving; just standing right in the middle of the road. My road, I might add, just outside my house. And here he is blocking my pathway as if he owned the road. Great. Now what do I do?

I really would like to get inside if you don't mind, I think. I need to get home. I need to get out of this horrible January cold; this dark. And he just stares at me.

Actually it's rather an alarming stare. Almost trance-like. Robotic. Can someone be both robotic and in a trance? Maybe not. But his head has started to swivel. So it's definitely more robot than trance.

The headlights of my car should be enough to tell him he is in danger of certain death and it may be a better idea to get out of the way, but he doesn't seem willing to recognise the fact that a large – well, actually a Honda Civic – car has come up the hill and he is standing on the dotted white line which, I might add, is there for a reason. It's not a runway. Nor are they (the lines) needed if I'm honest, the road is not exactly of avenue width. I know this because of the hooting every morning as the cars queue for their 'turn' to drive on. They are there to indicate which side of the road you are supposed to be on. And there isn't a choice. You can't hedge your bets, you idiot. You're not supposed to stand on them.

Now listen mister, I think to myself. (I daren't actually speak to him. You see, I haven't lived here long and the neighbours and me, well, we're still weighing each other up, if you know what I mean.) But I am wondering why he doesn't get the message that the middle of the road on a Friday night in January is not the best place to stand, unless of course you're awaiting certain death.

And then it occurs to me. Perhaps that's exactly what he is doing. Maybe he has decided to end it all. At which point he blinks. That's it then. He's definitely alive and maybe not in a trance because I know trance-like states mean no blinking. I know this because Robert what's-his-name played Jesus without blinking. Apparently he had to learn this skill in just a few days. I can't do it. I did try when, as a child, I was forced to watch Jesus of Nazareth by my holy family, and spent the time trying not to blink just like Mr P. All I managed was red eyes and a slimy face.

I haven't been drinking, you know. My head is absolutely clear. My problem is I have what people call a butterfly mind. I see something or someone and I go off into an imaginative romp. Same when I'm reading. I was on page 11 of Chesil Beach for nearly an hour last night. Completely trapped in the idea of Edward offering Florence a glazed cherry. I simply couldn't get past it. Why would he? And why glazed?

Now he's looking at me again. My engine revs a bit with my irritable foot. Nothing.

He doesn't look in the least apprehensive. He's still staring at me.

I'm not getting out. Anything could happen. But then suppose I'm causing a traffic jam? A glance in the mirror confirms that the entire road on this side of Whitstable is deserted and not even a dog is passing. Or a fox or... Actually, that's a good point. A fox would be good at this moment.

'You'd better watch out!' I shout through the windscreen, 'The fox'll get you if you don't go away!'

He turns his head sharply to the left. His left, my right. Then back to the front, then to the right. His right, my left. And every time he does so, he blinks.

But he doesn't move.

Now I start to consider what would happen if I stayed in the car all night. Maybe slept in it. I'm not getting out and I certainly can't touch him. Might catch something.

I so need to go to bed. It's been a long day, my day. Bet he hasn't had such a long day as I have. But the car cannot stay here. I need to move it. Maybe I can move round him. Maybe, if I'm really careful I can move past him so slowly and quietly. No revving. I could creep past him and then zoom into the drive and run for the door.

One thing is certain, I can't run him over.

He's staring again, like he knows what I'm thinking. Perhaps he does. Perhaps I should stop thinking. Perhaps I can pretend I've not seen him or that I'm waiting for someone.

I start to sing. Not a song as such but just a cheerful tune. My hands beat time on the steering wheel. I'm beginning to enjoy myself. I could actually spend the entire night singing and just wait for him to leave. But then what about the early morning traffic? All those cars queuing and hooting, those lorries bouncing down the road over the speed ramps, with no care for their suspension. They wouldn't be too pleased to see a mad woman snoring in the car. Definitely drunk, they would think. Daft old bint.

No, I can't let that happen. I need to move.

I grip the steering wheel and up the tempo of the tune; increase the volume so as not to hear the screams, apply some pressure to the clutch. The car bounds forward with an alarming lurch. Too much pressure on the clutch, clearly. My clutch control has never been my finest asset. 'You trying to kill us dear?' my father would ask in his kindly voice.

I look through the windscreen at the empty space, lit up starkly by the glare of headlamps. No more staring eyes. No more robotic head. Oh my God! He's under the car. Blood; gore; everything.

The singing ceases. Silence.

Handbrake on. Rear view mirror. Why does no-one come? Maybe a pedestrian or a cyclist could wander up? Why is no one up at this hour?

With a shaking hand I reach for the door handle. What happens next unnerves me so much I scream. A light comes on. But who has done that? A light? Who's shining a light on me? I've done nothing wrong. And then I see the car door is open. My door. Of my car. Opened by me. No monster; no terrorist. Me.

I really must calm down and take control of this situation. I place my foot carefully on the ground, breathe deeply and move past the bonnet with eyes tight shut trying to control my breathing and trying not to scream. I glance down at the carnage.

He is still blinking and staring at the bumper. Unharmed. Alive. No carnage then. No gore today.

And then I see on his left side there is something dragging on the ground. Like a badly fitting coat, there is a grey and white flap, a large coat flap minus the buttons, hanging useless beside him. It is a wing. His wing. And it doesn't work anymore.

He takes no notice of me. He may be embarrassed at this lack of Gull couture. Not a look, not a word. Just straight ahead with the glancing head and the staring eyes. Maybe it hurt to lose a wing; emotionally and sartorially. Maybe he is numb with pain. Maybe there is nothing for me to be scared of.

Lights wink at the top of the hill, forecasting another car driver intent on driving down the hill. I must move. We must move. He can't. My car can't. No contest then. I must pick him up and take him in.

Logic says run to the boot, get out your gloves, pick him up and leave him somewhere safe. Move the car out of the way, then decide.

Instinct says, run like hell, leave the car with the engine running! Go! Go! Go!

Logic wins.

I carry him gingerly to the doorstep. Run back to the car. Shut the door. Three point turn, always been good at these, 'turn on a sixpence, you can', my father used to say. Into the drive. Out of the car and wave 'sorry' to the perturbed man glaring at me through the passenger window. He moves on down the hill with a mournful shake of the head.

I stare at the empty space where the decision was made. Nothing there. Not even feathers.

I glance at my Gull. Now what?

On reflection, I have no idea why I used the possessive pronoun there. He was not mine. He was just a gull with a wing dragging on the ground, shaken – no, traumatised – by something; maybe a driver in a hurry. Maybe a fox. But he was alive. And I could not kill him so I had to save him. No such thing as a Gull ambulance or a Gull doctor. No, I was on my own with this.

When I say couldn't kill him, it does not mean that I hold any high moral position on this. I am not the Buddha. I am me. I could have thrown him into a hedge and hoped he would be killed by something else or I could have run him over. Actually, that's the point. I could not contemplate driving over flesh. All of my skin twitches at the thought and I heave with disgust.

The irony is I've always hated seagulls. As a child, I found the cry invigorating with a promise of adventure. Summer and holidays and swimming in the sea. But I soon learnt that, close up, they had mean faces and snarly curling beaks. And they never looked straight at you. It was as if they were trying to ignore you until your attention was elsewhere. Then they would swoop like bandits and take away your food, your fish and chips, your sausage, anything that the windswept promenade had not stolen already.

Now as a home owner, they had sought me out to leave their doo-doo on my windows, my car, my roof and definitely my doorstep. There was nothing to like about them, so why save one? I wasn't lonely. Didn't need a pet. And I hated seagulls. And yet, here he is two months on in his own hutch like a wingless rabbit and I share my fish with him.

He is, it is true, more appreciative of me now. He literally knows which side his bread is buttered and although we have not conversed, he has improved his temper and I mine. The wing that dragged has mended, not perfectly but enough for it to enable movement. He can't fold it away on his back like the other one but recently he's found a way of pulling it up with his beak and I place it on his back and tie it with a ribbon.

I have photographed this ingenuity and put it on Facebook. No likes yet. One comment. 'Are you okay?'

I run a film through my head of the day the news was broken to him. I play the Doctor in the film and we often play the scene over when there's no-one looking.

Me. 'You have to understand, my friend, that you are very unlikely to fly again.'

Silence.

Me. 'You've had a lucky escape and sooner or later you will be pain free, but you must never go out alone because someone will take advantage of you and you may not survive.'

Further silence. A tear glistens in the corner of my eye.

Me. 'But you're lucky to have someone who cares for you. You can live a good and simple life. But there will be no more travelling, I'm afraid. Here is where you must stay.'

Yes, I know, I get all the best lines and the glistening tear drop is actually Vaseline. But it would make a really great movie. He can't talk, so it's more of a solo. A monologue if you will. At least, that's what I thought.

The neighbours are friendly in a concerned sort of way. They pass by and wave when I'm out in the front cleaning the Gull hutch. When I had the brainwave about the ribbon for the wing, I noticed a slight quickening in their step and they seemed newly determined to get to Harbour Street. My friendliest neighbour pretends nothing has happened but she stays at the top of the drive now and doesn't come to the door.

Her husband looks at me and smiles in a way that can only be called pity. But I don't mind any of this because I realise something deeply profound has happened.

I am a saviour. Not of the world or mankind or even man, but I have saved a living being and that is good. And the fact is that this creature, which I have always despised, I can look upon differently without judgement and see that we are all equal in the eyes of... well, maybe not God or the neighbours but definitely the RSPCA. I must be saving them thousands.

One thing bothers me, however. The night I picked him up and took him in. The night I saved him from Death, if you will. I heard him say, 'What kept you?'

Now, be honest. You were going to turn the page at this point, weren't you? You were going on to the next story. This is too ridiculous for words, you're thinking.

Well, dear reader, before you judge me or indeed my Gull, – there, I've done it again. My Gull – Well, anyway, before you bring all your judgement to bear, think about this.

In all the stories you've ever heard concerning animals and birds, when was the time you questioned that they could speak? That ruddy goody two shoes spider in Charlotte's Web for example. She used to write the script in her web, never mind speak. And did you ever question that? Did Disney? No.

And the Gull in Watership Down. He was German or something. 'Perfect Landing' said with a well-practised guttural accent. Did you laugh at that? Of course you did! But you never said, 'No this is not possible.'

Well, I am here to tell you that my Gull sounds very South London. And rather rude. But I definitely heard him say that. 'What kept you?'

I suppose he had a point. I had taken my time, though part of me said I should have left him there. But then the oncoming car was zooming down the hill and I did need to be pretty speedy in the disposal of bird and the moving of car. So I just took him and then I didn't know where to put him so I left him on the step.

He still didn't look at me even then. He just stood on those stupid spindly legs of his with his stupid straight ahead feet and waited some more. I told him he couldn't come in and would have to wait while I sorted out a hutch. In the meantime, he had to stay in one of the bins. He had no idea of the context of rubbish of course so didn't mind too much. In fact, I think I heard 'Okay. Thanks.'

I went to the pet shop the next day and found one the right size.

'Is it the first time you've kept a rabbit?' she asked.

I stared at her, not quite seeing the point of the question.

'Because if so, you will probably find one of these useful.' A book entitled 'Caring for your Rabbit' was thrust into my hand. I smiled and said thank you. 'Do you have one for seagulls?' was simply not the question to be asking just now. So I thanked her and slowly struggled with the hutch back up the hill and put it next to the bin.

So now he has a hutch by the front door and the postman always asks after him and especially the ribbon situation. If I let him, he'd stay for hours chatting about matters seagull. It's almost as if he's worried about me.

But the Gull has made it clear that his company is not welcomed for any longer than it takes to deliver my post. 'Thought he'd never go,' I heard him say the first time.

And after that he practised his robot stare to a knot in the wood in the rabbit hutch. The postman soon got the message.

And our relationship – me and my Gull, I mean – our relationship has changed since the ribbon intervention. There is a definite change there. Actually I'm thinking of getting him a lead from the pet shop but as yet I haven't found a collar that is small enough. And I'm not ready to take a seagull into the high street to have a collar fitted. Not until I'm over the ribbon comments. We like the ribbon and that's all that matters.

By the way, 'On Chesil Beach' doesn't contain one single seagull reference. What kind of story is that?

Philadelphia and the Sea

By Lin White

Based on a true story

Boston, Massachusetts, 1930

William held tight to his grandmother's hand. 'Why do we come to the harbour so often?' he asked, looking up at her.

'Look at all those people. Some know exactly what to do, and others are stepping off the ship in this country for their first time ever.' Philadelphia waved her hand over the crowds disembarking the passenger ship and heading towards the harbour offices.

William pointed to a boy and girl who stood holding hands, a single bag on the quayside between them. They were looking around, as though lost. 'They're only as old as I am, and they're on their own.'

'That could almost be your Great-Aunt and Great-Uncle. They were about that age when they first sailed over here.' The years faded away as Philadelphia looked down at the young pair and thought back to that time, all those years ago, when she had met her young brother and sister at the docks.

'Have you ever been on a ship, Grandmother?' Her grandson's soft voice brought her back to the present.

'Oh yes. Many times. And my father worked on boats, but none so big as these.'

William gazed up, his eyes wide. 'Are you very rich, Grandmother?' he asked, and she laughed.

Leading him to a nearby bench, she pulled him down beside her. 'I was very poor when I was your age,' she said. 'I remember standing in the harbour where my father worked, looking at the fishing boats, and asking him which one went to America.'

Whitstable, 1878

'Father, which boat is the one that goes to America?' Philly stared at the huddle of boats moored up at Whitstable quay.

Father laughed loud and long. 'These don't go to America,' he said. 'They're far too small. Even the biggest of these only goes as far as London, with the day's catch of oysters and whelks.'

Philly's face fell. 'But Mother said that one day we would get on a boat and go to America.'

Father turned and held both her small, delicate hands in his big rough ones. 'Mother is full of dreams,' he said. 'And she shouldn't be filling your head with them.' As he saw her eyes fill with tears, he softened his voice. 'She heard tell of a beautiful city called Philadelphia once, and that's why she chose your name. She has ideas that one day we'll go to America and make lots of money and have whatever we want, but it costs a lot of money to get there. It's not for the likes of us.'

Philly stuck her jaw out. 'One day I'll go there,' she declared. 'And I'll make my fortune, and send it all home to you, so you can come out there too.'

Her father hoisted her up onto his shoulders. 'I look forward to it, young Philly,' he said, as she squealed with delight. 'But now we need to get home, and see if your mother has had that baby yet.'

At the age of eight, Philly was small but strong. Edwin, her older brother, was determined to follow in their father's footsteps and work as a fisherman, and spent all his time at the harbour or the fishing huts when he was not studying, but Philly would clean and cook and help her mother with Nathaniel, her younger brother. Now Mother was expecting another baby. Philly hoped it would be a girl. It would be nice to have a little baby sister to play with and care for.

Their little terraced house in Albert Street was only a couple of minutes away from the harbour. Her father put her back down on the ground, and she skipped merrily along, holding his hand. When they reached home, Auntie Mabel let them in the door, pressing a finger to her lips for quiet. 'You have a lovely little baby girl,' she told Father. He beamed and swung Philly round.

At first Philly enjoyed helping with baby Charlotte, but she started to notice that her father seemed angry and quiet. He would say very little when he came home, and would eat and head straight for bed. Mother would watch him leave the room, with a sad look on her face. One day, Philly came home from school at lunchtime to find her father sitting in a chair by the fire, his face thin and miserable. 'Your father is ill,' Mother said gently. But Father was never ill. How would they get money for food if he couldn't work?

Over the next few weeks, Philly would think back to that afternoon at the harbour as the last time she had been truly happy. Since then, she had been busy caring for Charlotte, watching her mother nurse her father and then fall sick herself, and then came the news she had been dreading: she came home from school at the end of the day, holding tightly to Nathaniel's hand, to find the house full of people, some of them crying. 'It's your father,' Auntie Mabel told her. 'I'm sorry, children, but you must be brave.'

Edwin stood proudly at the door. 'I'm the man of the house, now,' he declared to Philly. 'I'll look after you. I'm going to get a job and earn enough money to keep us all.'

But jobs for twelve-year-olds did not pay well, and he still had to attend school, and although the men at the harbour did their best to help the family out, still Philly found it harder and harder to provide nourishing meals for the family. Her mother was very sick as well, by this time, and one day there was even worse news.

'We need to go into the workhouse for a while,' Mother said weakly, as the children gathered around her. 'They will nurse me and provide for you. We cannot be a burden to Aunt Mabel and Uncle Ron any longer. They have their own children to feed and care for.'

'I can do it all,' Philly whispered, tears streaming down her face. 'Am I not good enough, Mother? I'll try harder, I promise.'

Mother reached forward and cupped her daughter's face in her trembling hands. 'You are doing wonderfully, my little Philly,' she said. 'But I cannot care for you as I should, and they will see you are kept safe. Be happy, my children, and one day perhaps you will all get on one of those big ships and sail away to a new land, where you can have all that I want you to have but cannot give you.'

Philly shivered when she first saw the workhouse just outside Herne village. It was spoken of in whispers by everyone she knew; the greatest fear of the poorest in the community was being taken into the workhouse. She saw the boys taken away to another room, and then she, Charlotte and their mother were made to scrub themselves as clean as they could in filthy, cold water, and then were given clothes to wear. They were threadbare, and fitted poorly, but at least they were warm.

The children soon settled into life in the workhouse. Mother was taken into the hospital ward, where Philly helped out whenever she could. Charlotte was in the nursery room, a sad place with several children and few toys. The boys were all kept in the boys' ward, and saw the girls only briefly at mealtimes, when talking was forbidden, or on a Sunday afternoon, when they were all allowed to gather briefly in one of the visiting rooms.

Mother died within a couple of weeks of them entering the workhouse. By that time, Philly had grown used to the hard work and lack of comfort. She had made a friend, Mary, and the time they would spend whispering together while washing and repairing the clothes became precious to her. She studied hard in the workhouse school, and did her chores in the laundry, and helped out in the hospital and nursery whenever she could.

As Charlotte grew older and joined them in the girls' ward, Philly started helping in the kitchens instead. She would help make the bread and broth for the inmates, and cups of tea for the elderly people in the sick ward, and she also cooked for the Master and Mistress, and for the porter and the teacher and the other staff, who all lived in. She and Mary would chat quietly as they worked, under the stern eye of Mrs Watford, the cook. Mary loved to hear Philly's stories of the wonderful city in a different country that shared her name, and together they dreamed of running away for a fresh start in a new place.

One day, a rich lady donated some periodicals to the workhouse, and in one of them Philly found pictures of the city called Philadelphia. She hid the periodical under her mattress, and would gaze it when she felt miserable. 'One day I'll go there,' she would say to herself.

Whenever Philly and Charlotte met the boys, Edwin swore that he still intended to get a job and support them all, so that they could live together again, but there was no sign of it, until the day that he proudly announced that the workhouse had found him an apprenticeship in the town, working for a carpenter. For the first few weeks he still visited every Sunday afternoon, but one week he didn't turn up.

The next day, Philly was trying to hide her tears as she stirred the broth for dinner. Mrs Watford saw her. 'You upset about your big brother running off?' she asked her.

'What do you mean?' Philly had heard nothing about Edwin, and was worried that something had happened to him.

'Your no-good brother has run off from his apprenticeship,' the cook snorted. 'Couldn't stand the hard work. He'll get nowhere in life with that attitude.'

Philly felt her heart would break. How could he run off and abandon them? She turned to Mary in despair, but Mary had bad news for her too. 'My father's family in Sussex have called for me,' she said. 'I'm to be moved to a workhouse near where they live.'

Even when their teacher arranged for them to all travel to Whitstable to paddle on the beach, as a break from studying their reading and writing, Philly found she could not enjoy the sea. She stood gazing out at the big ships. She was old enough now to understand that the ships that would go over to America were far bigger, but she had given up any hope of ever being on one.

When she had her fourteenth birthday, a few months later, the workhouse found her a job as a cook in a big house in Whitstable. By now she was used to cooking fine meals, and settled to working well, although she missed all the other girls in the workhouse. Her favourite time was when she visited the harbour at Whitstable, and could again see and hear the fishermen at work and see the ships. Several of the fishermen remembered her and her family, and greeted her cheerfully. She would wave, give one last longing look out to sea, and then visit the stall where she could buy fish for that evening's dinner.

Every Sunday after church she made the long walk to visit her brother and sister in the workhouse. Charlotte would cling to her and cry, and Nathaniel would ask about Edwin, and every time she had to say that no, she had heard nothing about Edwin, and yes, she was saving up her money to support them and one day they would be together again.

Then one Sunday afternoon, as she was leaving the workhouse, a voice called to her. She looked over to the far side of the road, and to her shock she saw Mary standing there. 'What are you doing here?' she asked her.

Mary gave a broad smile, and hugged her. 'I'm here with a message from Edwin,' she said. 'Would you believe, he's in Canada!'

'Canada?' Philly had heard of the place, far away across the sea, but what was Edwin doing there and how had he got there?

'He wants us to go out and join him,' Mary confided, slipping her arm through her friend's. 'There's a company who sends young people like us out to America and Canada for a new life. He's sent for me and wants you to come as well.'

Philly gasped in shock. Go to Canada? It couldn't possibly happen.

But it did. There were plans to make and papers to sign, but within a few weeks she and Mary were standing on the deck of a ship sailing out to Nova Scotia, where Edwin met them. He and Mary were married within a few days of their arrival, and set up home in a small house in the town. Philly lived with them. Edwin had a good job out there, helping to build all the new houses that were needed for the immigrants, and he was making good money. Philly and Mary both had jobs, until Mary became pregnant and gave birth to a baby girl, whom they called Philadelphia after her aunt.

Edwin sent money to the workhouse in England regularly to support Nathaniel and Charlotte, and arranged for them to live in a local boarding house instead of living in. One day, Philly found Edwin going through a list of bills, trying to work out how to afford to pay them and still send the money to the workhouse. 'Why don't you send for them to live here?' she asked him.

'Philly, you're very clever,' he declared, after careful consideration. Letters were sent, arrangements were made, and a few months later Philly and Mary stood on the quay waiting for the ship to dock, bringing twelve year old Nathaniel and ten year old Charlotte.

They stayed in Canada for another year, with Edwin learning his trade and making good money, but he missed England, and before long he and Mary were talking about returning across the sea. Philly travelled with them, and joined them in a tiny house on Herne Bay seafront, but she missed the bustle of Nova Scotia, and found herself once again spending her free time on the beach gazing out at the big ships. Eventually she had saved enough money to travel back out, this time disembarking at Boston harbour. Within a year of landing there, she had fallen in love with a man named William, and they were married.

When they were looking for somewhere to live, they visited Philadelphia, and Philly exclaimed over the sights she recognised from the old periodical she had read so many times, but in the end it was too far from the sea for her, and they settled in Boston.

There they lived very happily, raising their two children and then helping with the grandchildren. Charlotte and Nathaniel both returned as well, and settled in San Fanscisco, while Edwin stayed in Herne. Mary ran the post office at Eddington, with little Philly's help, while Edwin's customers included the workhouse where he had spent time as a child.

Philly wrote regularly to her brothers and sister, visited them occasionally, and liked nothing better than to take her young grandson to the harbour, watch the ships come sailing in with their passengers, and remember the times on the beach at Whitstable, where she had dreamed of a better life in a new country.

The Tree With Pleading Hands

By Phillip Mind

I have been watching her. I have been worried for her ever since she found me. Dead. On my bedroom floor. Not a pretty sight. She cleaned up as best she could. The bottles, the fag ends and ash, the left-over meals. The decay. Flies.

So this one day. A few months later.

The sun shone. She started the day sitting outside a café eating breakfast, looking out over the passing crowds, the sunshine washing over her ridiculous sunglasses, shiny business suit, the white blouse, the bobbed dark hair and the designer jewellery. Ostentatious, if you want my opinion. Difficult to age, looks somewhere over forty not near fifty, executive, aspirational type, looks after herself.

She wouldn't believe it. But she's a type.

It looked like she joked with the waiter. He probably thought she was a right old tart. Then she played with her phone. They do that a lot now, her type. Then she walked around the corner past Westminster Cathedral, into the glass and steel office block. Steel, glass and concrete, not a brick in sight.

The sun was low and shining and there would be a brass band in the park later. More my cup of tea. I slipped into a deckchair. I needed to doze. I needed the weight off my feet. Let the world go by. One eye open, one eye shut. I knew where she was, what she was doing.

I am sorry to say I watch others too. I know more about

them all now than I ever did before. Their secret lives. I try not to intrude but sometimes you see things. Sometimes it is small acts of love and kindness, which I appreciate. But it isn't always like that. We aren't always what we seem.

I dozed the day away feet up and then made my way to Victoria Street. I saw her come past just after 5 o'clock. It wasn't easy to spot her in the rush but I have a feeling for her now. So to say I saw her is misleading. I felt something. It takes a while, creeps up on you but then you sense it. Friday night, everyone keen to get somewhere, to do something, to live a little. I followed her down into Victoria station. An uneventful day.

I took some photos early this morning of the city with the Spring sun shining. I put one on Facebook. Looking now, he hasn't liked it – that's strange. The king of Facebook, princeling of the social media. His battery must be dead. Dead. And I thought of that day. Opening the door. Mum. I breathe through it. Try and get back to the now. Breathe.

I text to let him know I'm on the train – home at 7 darling weekend rock x. Trying to summon something but honestly I am still grieving. Although I do a passable job of hiding it. Masking.

Nothing really to prepare me for what takes place. When the train arrives in Whitstable, I watch her step. I follow her as she walks from the station down Cromwell Road towards home. There is this blinding red and orange sunset, a proper decent Sheppey sky. I am almost tempted to head off towards the beach and watch it set, sit by the Neptune, look at them watching the sun disappear beyond the horizon. Not many of them will be up gazing on its rise. Funny that.

His car isn't in the drive, which is strange, and no reply to my text. I call as I enter the hall. Its dusk but there are no lights on, nothing, the air in the house is chill. There is an envelope on the table, propped up, so that it can't be missed, my name on the front in his handwriting.

I pick it up and sit on the sofa. My mind has already started to race, although I feel like I am studying myself. I am ahead of the letter, anticipating its contents and scanning, not examining it carefully. 'Fresh start' and 'not the husband you want me to be' and 'I will always love you as the mother of my children but I can't love you as a husband any more'. Where are they? Where is my little Ben?

Something bad has happened. I can see it. See it in her face. The house is normally alive at this time of night with the boys and their toings and froings, with Paul busying, TVs, music, everything and everyone jostling for attention. Not tonight. The house is dead. She is reading a letter, that much I can make out. She is frowning. Vexed. She stands up and walks to the bedroom. I lose sight of her.

I nip round the back into the garden. She is sitting on the bed, head in her hands. She stands up, removes her phone, glances at it and launches it across the room. I know more than I let on. I have watched Paul. I am not overly fond of him and maybe I shouldn't have done the looking. But it just so happened I followed him longer than strictly necessary, not out of idle curiosity but just to – well, observe. But look what I observed. Gallivanting. Not all good and I wished I had stuck with her, where I belong. I am jumping about here a bit.

She has her eyes shut, looks like she is breathing deeply, long hard sobbing breaths. She is crying and I feel powerless, wanting to reach out so desperately.

I walk round the house. Room to room. Desperate. Hoping it's a joke. It's oppressive. Ben. Where has he taken him? When will I see him? I need some space to be out of here. If I run I can think, decide what to do, how to respond, make a plan, try not to go mental. A long run, tire myself out. Ben is safe, he loves Ben. I meditate, or try to, calm my mind, breathe and empty the thoughts, let them go, centring. Try not to think of my boys, where he has taken them, what he must be thinking. My little boy. I am howling. I try to stop. Deep breaths.

I am not an idiot. I can put two plus two together. I had seen this coming. Sometimes Paul looked sad, unhappy with things. The absent look when I mentioned the future. I start to shake, there is a lot to react to and it's shredding in my mind. Just not the way I imagined it. I call him. Nothing. To voicemail. I call again. Straight to voicemail. You fucking bastard. I want to know where my child is. I should know. It's not fair to just do this, take him away. It will hurt him.

I can't bear my own agitation and run out of the house, head over the dyke running, across the golf course, casting towards the beach; it's dark now, I stride.

I spot him ahead in summer shorts, a beach bag, over one shoulder, the one the boys chose, his red hair under a hat keeping the sun off his skin, the same t-shirt, misshapen with holes. He is pushing the buggy with a little boy holding onto it, they are chatting. It's Ben. I can see by his wild gestures that Ben is speaking in his way where everything is epic or awesome. And Paul is laughing geeing him up. My Paul. My Ben.

It's not him though. And it's not Ben. It's almost dark. Too dark to notice anything. Inky.

I run onto the beach past Peter Cushing's house. He is standing on the beach in those battered yellow swimming trunks waving, encouraging me to swim in from the sea, a beckoning wave, and then folding his arms before turning and marching back up the beach. I put my head down into the water and begin propelling myself back to the beach, turning for air, into the red, taking in as little breath as possible, swimming hard. Into the shallows I run, catching him before he reaches our little camp of towels and spades.

Got you! I grab him. I laugh.

He pulls away. Get off, you're freezing. And for chrissake you have been in the sea for bloody ages. At one point we couldn't even see you. Ben was worried.

Little moments that pass by noticed cumulating as a feeling, an intuition, a worry about loss. Tiny gestures mounting until the gesture is etched into the rock and then the future is carved. A tape loop running in my head.

I have been watching her for a few months now. So I know the routes she takes when she runs – she's a creature of habit.

I amble down to the beach. There's a lovely little shelter just by the tennis courts – you can look out and survey the sea. It will take me a while to get down there. Better than hanging round at her house. Got to maintain eyes on her, make sure she doesn't overreact, watch for the signs.

I run into the harbour. We came down here a few weeks ago, a Friday late at night. He ran off the path, without a word, and headed down the beach to the sea. I could make out the bitter crunch of his steps on the pebbles and through the darkness make out his shape shifting and bobbing. Peering into the night, it looked like he was skipping. At the water's edge, he span, his arms wide apart, spinning, around, head tilted up to the stars. A star gazer. Not like my old dad, a real man, who could navigate by the stars.

As I run I can feel my eyes stinging, images playing in my head, the tightness in my chest that I know I will live with for months, the dryness in my mouth and the emotion so near the surface, bubbling somewhere volcanic. But it's okay because I am running, air in my lungs, and blood simply coursing in my veins.

But the run won't last. I will have to turn and head for home, but it isn't a home now, just a place where a woman lives, a woman whose husband walked out one day, who maybe feared his wife or feared for himself or who just fell out of love and felt old so much, so raw that there was no time for talk, no shall we try to save it, no argument or debate.

I head past the Hotel Continental, relentless in the rhythm, the pace, glancing right to see people gathered around tables, couples leaning into each other's gaze, groups of friends leaning back, all easy in their world, not counting their breath, not watching their stride, not blinking back a tape loop. Not in a reel.

It's a relief to head out into the darkness past the Street, just the ambient light from the top of Tankerton slopes casting shadows. The tide is out, you can smell the sea, the rotting oysters, seagulls squawking mindlessly. I pick up more pace, lengthen the stride, thinking about the seagulls, and how they create a mess and then

*move on. I imagine myself half woman, half seagull. Everything
will be like this now. This will be the prism. This will be the optic.
I can see the orange lights of Herne Bay twinkling. It's six miles
there and back but really what else is there on such a night?*

With the watching, you have to exercise patience. I can sit
and wait. I have learnt that. Be patient. I would say that to her,
hold your horses, but would she? Would she hell! Take starting
the car up, where to, guvnor, don't spare the horses. Racing
through the gears like Jackie Stewart. Who do you think I
am? Stirling Moss. I am. Mrs Moss to you. I am the world
champion. Good afternoon, Officer, yes, Mrs Stirling Moss.
Happy days. She could run her mouth off when she wanted to.

She'll come back. She'll come back safe. You have to think
that. No good if you don't. The worry would overwhelm
you. She won't run into the sea, she won't drown, the sea
smashing her body and her washing up bloated in bloody
Margate. Good grief, she wouldn't but it runs through your
mind. Those thoughts. The worst. The very worst. And the
downright dreadful. Best not to dwell on it. Rumination, not
a word I approve of.

A handsome man, Paul, that's what people would say
when he was a young man. The red hair, the curls, the way in
summer beads of perspiration would break out above his lips
and strands of hair would cling to the back of his neck. And
the talk, the voice, always conducting an inquiry. You could
almost feel him searching you for meaning. A philosophical
type.

She would mock it. Too quick to mock even then. Philosophy,
I am not sure I think of it at all. Who are your philosophical
friends?

She wouldn't let him be the cleverest person in the room,
fearful, I thought, of his power, the simplicity, the never
any pretence, just the eyes piercing you. He would have a
drink even then – whisky and water. Unusual for a seven-
teen-year-old boy. Finding a joke in it. A pair of pints, and a
pair of whiskies. Chin bloody chin.

Truth is, she could get lost. She should be back round. She can't run through the night. The bloody relentless running. When she was ten years old the kids in the road where we lived started running round the block, who can do the most laps, one by one dropping off, until it was just her. But she wouldn't stop, it wasn't enough just to beat them, and the other kids encouraged her, a few parents out in their gardens, washing cars on the drives, gawping; funny girl, they thought and she kept on. Lap after bloody lap and dusk began to fall.

In the end, her father came out. As she came past he cast her that look. It said come in now. But she swerved past him. Her face was a picture, she made it look effortless, the shimmy, dropping one shoulder, selling him the dummy. He turned around and marched inside – so much for the big rugby man. She kept going, something bloody minded, stubborn, obstinate, people lost interest. No one there to see her stop. Just the glare as she passed him by in the living room.

My head is whirring. The running can't still it or drive out the memories. I can't stop thinking about my little Ben. Where is he? Images of him come flooding in like I am sifting through a photo album. Images of Paul in a black leather jacket and beret in the Foret de Fountainebleau, posing hard-edged. Fetch me a gun so that you can shoot me down in cold blood and make me a resistance hero, an icon for future generations. Go on, shoot.

How am I going to erase all this stuff, how am I going to clear out my mind, how I am going to empty out? I stop. Purely out of the overwhelming futility. I should make calls, track him down.

Why I am out here running? It is the worst thing to do but I can't just can't keep running. I walk down to the beach and beyond it towards the sea, my trainers sinking into the mud, slipping on the stones, the rocks, the boulders, the debris, the cold water soaking through.

I reach the sea's edge and splinter, kneel down, the mud is cold, the stones punishing my shins. I plant my pleading hands into the brackish water, it's icy and I scream.

I scream out, unashamed, the effort ripping into my own

throat. And then I sob, kneeling, leaning forward, convulsing, pleading hands into the mud disturbing the stones, thinking let it wash over me, let it wash; and the waves just lap uselessly, harmlessly, gently, one lapping wave then after that another wave lapping softly. In a while, I'll lift myself up, just not right now.

They say you can't help from our side – just by looking. And I see their bloody point – I can't stay in the shelter all night like some lady tramp. Truth is, I am worried now. She always comes back this way. So I start to walk. It's a dark night but clear. You can see the lights on the island and right across to Southend, maybe that's Canvey Island. The chances of coming across her are slim. But that's not the point. You need to be out there looking.

It's just me, your dead mum, looking, scanning, listening for something, checking the obvious places, the benches, the walls, the decks, the places where if you needed a breather you could take one. I have patience but it is like pushing a rock up a hill. I sit on the wall by the Seaview Caravan Park. Nice place for a holiday, sea just by you over the sea wall, nice clubhouse, friendly.

I wait. I could go back to the house to see if she has showed up. Truth be told, I am angry. Let down. I won't use words but if I'd have known this was coming, I would have made more of an effort myself. I am at a loss now. There's no sight of her. She could have looped round, that sixth sense has maybe escaped me.

It's not late. Not too late to see, not too late to investigate.

I catch the bus over to Canterbury. Sit upstairs, there's light enough to see the trees. In the autumn, their pleading hands, raised up in supplication, gasping for oxygen, begging for a breath, taking it in.

There's an advert on the side – for the triangle. Herne Bay, Whitstable, Canterbury. The triangle. People get on those buses and never get off. Never get off. It's a mystery over-shadowed by the more celebrated triangle in Bermuda. Or she would say is that to throw us off the scent? Anyway, she'd get the explorer pass; you pay your money, you take your chances, in the Triangle.

There's only so many places he can be. I take an educated guess based on past observations and retrace my steps. The rooms are tiny but it's a clean and modern flat. I let myself in. It's all about love, you see. The love for the child lets you in. Gives you the permission.

Paul is sitting on a stool at a breakfast bar, phone on the counter, rounded shoulders sagging. Straighten out, love. He is smoking a ciggy, fingers fidgeting with it, edgy. You silly boy, look at you. You have got yourself in a right state.

I sit down right smack bang opposite him. It's hard to contain the anger. He exhales, blowing the smoke steadily away from his face, slowly, gently, tilting upwards to the ceiling. His eyes are red, blotchy face, he's had a good cry today. A weak man.

Truth is, I am a forgiving, Christian type. And yet – and I surprise myself – with everything I have, I summon a breath wheezing. I blow the smoke hard as hell back towards him into his eyes. He's startled, puzzled even.

I can see the smoke; it's stinging. She's my little girl after all. We watch for our own.

Peter Cushing Never Played Dracula

by David Williamson

'Sir, where are you?' said Radford excitedly. 'You really need to get here soon.'

Inspector Collins was sitting in the squad car with his foot resting lazily on the clutch. 'I'll be there as soon as I can, just held up on the High Street. Won't be long, Radford.' Collins flipped his mobile onto the passenger seat and sighed heavily. Radford had a tendency to get a little over-excited at times. Everything was 'urgent' with Radford; nice lad, but overly keen. This message from Radford to meet him urgently by the East Quay beach had better not be another waste of time. The week before, Radford had sent a call out to all cars about a traffic incident over in Herne Bay. Three squad cars had arrived, to find the so-called urgent incident turned out to be nothing more than a large field mouse laid on its back near the zebra crossing on Tankerton Road. What a waste of Police resources. Yeah, he must have a quiet word with Radford sometime.

Just what the hell was holding up the traffic? Collins craned his neck out of the car window to look down the High Street, but the bus in front of him was partially blocking his view. He opened the door of the car and looked back up the street. Some idiot had double-parked outside the bank blocking the traffic.

They were always doing it, jumping out of their cars to rush to the ATM. So bloody inconsiderate. He looked behind him and there was a tailback of twenty cars, maybe more. He got back in the car and decided to sit it out. The High Street was getting busy with day-tripping DFLs (Down from London) ambling up the street and peering into the windows of the shops and spending good money on old junk that had been given a lick of Farrow & Ball. They had money to burn, did those DFLs. Still, it kept the local economy ticking over. Margate would kill for half the DFLs they got here. His mobile rang again.

'Sir, it's me, just wondering where you are.'

'For Christ's sake, Radford, I'm still stuck in traffic. I'll be there as soon as I can.'

'Okay Sir, I'll see you when you get here.'

'Yes, obviously.'

He shook his head in disbelief. There must be more to life than this. He looked through his windscreen at the back of the bus in front. There was an advert for the new Oyster Land Visitor Centre.

OYSTER LAND
Fun for all the family – so much to see and do!

Learn about the history of the oyster from Roman times to the present day
Oyster-opening demonstrations daily
Decorate your own oyster shell
Meet Cap'n Shelly and his merry band of oyster-catchers
See Augustus – Europe's oldest oyster
Pearl Harbour – children's oyster-petting zone
Gift shop and Cap'n Shelly's tea room
Early bookings recommended!

Collins muttered to himself, 'How the hell do they know that Augustus is Europe's oldest oyster? Did they ask him? Excuse me, how old are you? What's that you say? Two thousand years old? Really? That's fantastic. Hey, Augustus, how would you like to come and work at Oysterland? Flexible hours, good pension plan too.' Good grief, a visitor centre about oysters, that'll never catch on. There had been a local entrepreneur who had flopped last year with something equally ridiculous: 'Peter Cushing's Fang-Tastic Museum.' A dozen or so shop dummies dressed up to look like Dracula. Five quid to get in. God knows what Peter Cushing, famous son of Whitstable, would have made of it. He'd be rolling over in his silk-lined coffin probably! Peter Cushing didn't even play Dracula; they got that wrong for a start. He always played the kindly doctor or the local vicar. He was the one saving all those pretty virgins that every Victorian village seemed to have in abundance, not sucking their blood. People should get their facts right before setting up a visitor attraction like that. Anyhow, what did it matter, it closed down after a couple of weeks. Now, if that guy had any sense he should have forgotten about Dracula and opened up a coffee shop instead. That's what the DFLs want most, coffee shops and over-priced charcuteries and pop-up shops selling sweaty old vintage clothes.

The bus in front rattled and spurted out a thick mass of black smoke from its exhaust; the traffic was moving again. He got as far as Wheeler's Seafood Shop when there was another halt in the traffic. 'Now what? Another field mouse? A large wasp?' He wound down his window but couldn't see past the bus. He got out and walked down the centre of the road to see what was going on. Cars were beeping their horns impatiently and other drivers were getting out of their cars to see what was happening. A Range Rover had stopped in the middle of the road near the junction, the worst place in all the town to stop. A woman sat behind the wheel of the van, seemingly oblivious to the tailback she was causing. Collins indicated to her to wind down her window.

'Hello Madam, have you broken down?'

She looked down at him vaguely. 'No, why?'

'Because you're clogging up the High Street. Why have you stopped?'

She smiled apologetically. 'Sorry, I was just looking at the sign in the Estate Agent's window – they're offering valuations on houses until the end of September at special rates.'

'What?'

She pointed over to the Estate Agents window. 'See for yourself – valuations on your house at only 63% commission, offer ends soon.'

Collins scratched his chin. 'Fine, that's great, now I must ask you to move on please.'

'Why? Who are you?'

'Who am I … ?' It was at moments like this he questioned whether some members of the public inhabited the same planet. Surely his police uniform might have given just a hint that he was an officer of the law. He looked around him to see if anyone was nearby to witness the absurdity of this. No one was taking any notice.

'I'm a police officer, Madam.'

'Prove it – where's your ID?'

'Pardon? Look, I haven't got time for this, just move it, OK?'

'Before I do, what are you going to do about that large tarantula on top of the Estate Agent's roof?' She pointed upwards. Collins followed her finger. It was true. A large tarantula, maybe a metre across, was making its way over the tiles of the sloping roof towards Wheeler's Seafood Restaurant. It was no big deal.

'Well Madam, if it is such a concern to you, I suggest you wind up your window, move your car, and stop holding up the traffic. Thank you for your co-operation. Goodbye.'

He turned and headed back to the squad car, shaking his head as he did so. 'This bloody little town,' he muttered to himself. 'Full of nutters.' He opened the door and slumped in his seat.

'For Christ's sake! Who are you?'

There was an elderly woman sat in the passenger seat next to him with a shopping bag on her lap.

'Your phone's been ringing, Officer.'

'What?'

'Your mobile, it's been ringing. You left here on this seat, any one could have taken it. Lucky for you it was me.'

'Never mind that, what are you doing in my car?'

'Oh, I just saw the police car and thought that as you seemed to be heading up the High Street you might give me a lift to Tankerton. I forgot my bus pass, you see, and I've only a few pence left in my purse; silly me, spent too much at Morrison's.'

At that moment the phone rang.

'Hello Sir, it's Constable Radford here... '

'Yes Radford, I guessed as much, what is it?'

'Just wondering when you would be getting here, Sir.'

'In a minute, okay? In a minute I'll be there.'

He threw the mobile over his shoulder onto the back seat. The old woman scowled at him.

'You'll break it throwing it like that. Things come far too easy these days. You'd think twice if it was your own money and not taxpayer's money who'd bought that thing. Them mobiles don't come cheap. I asked my nephew Simon to get me one but when he told me how much they were I told him to forget it. Anyhow, he said I needed one so he could keep track of me and bought one for me as a present. He's such a kind boy. Do you know Simon?'

'Simon? I can't say I do... '

'You must do, he lives in Whitstable. He has blond hair and glasses.'

'I'll need a better ID than that, I'm afraid. Anyhow, I'm sorry, Madam, but I must ask you to get out.'

'Well that's very mean I must say. Where are you going?'

'To the beach, by the East Quay.'

'Ooh good, well you can drive me as far as that then and I'll get a taxi outside the Ice-Skating rink.'

'I thought you didn't have any money, Madam.'

A car behind sounded its horn, quickly followed by a succession of more car horns. Collins looked up. The road in front of him was now clear.

'Okay, I'll take you as far as the Quay, then you'll have to get out.'

They got a hundred yards along the road when the old lady suddenly shrieked. 'Oh dear, oh no! We'll have to go back to Morrison's, I've forgotten something.'

'I can't madam; we're in a one-way system.'

'Oh! How could I be so forgetful?' she said with genuine panic.

'Why, what have you forgotten?'

'My Zimmer frame.'

'Come again?'

'I left my Zimmer frame by the checkouts. Oh, dear.'

This didn't quite compute with Collins.

'So… how did you manage to walk up the High Street and get in this car?'

'Well, I don't really need that old zimmer, I suppose, but it would be a shame to have it stolen.'

'I doubt that would happen, Madam.'

You never know who's around these days. Teenagers, hooligans, all them foreigners we've got living here these days. Turn your head for one second and it could be halfway to Romania or Afghanistan before you know it. I bet they don't have zimmers where they come from. No NHS in them places you know. I'll tell you what, Officer, why don't you just take me home and I'll drive back into town later this afternoon and collect it. Hope there's no big birds or tarantulas on the road though. Bloody nuisances they are. I had a massive praying mantis in me back garden the other day. Horrible green-looking thing it was. I had just put me laundry on the washing line and I spotted it from the dining room window nibbling on me knickers and me orthopaedic tights that I had just pegged out. I came rushing out of the back door with me sweeping brush and chased the bugger right off. Bloody nuisances. Never had 'em in my day. If Peter Cushing was still alive he'd soon scare the buggers off with his big fangs and all that. They'd all move on to Broadstairs or back to Romania or somewhere else. Yes, just take me home, that'll be best, I'll drive back into town later. Ooh, wait though. Maybe I could ask Simon to take me. Do you know Simon? My nephew? He's got short black hair and a beard and lives in town. That beard he's grown doesn't suit him one bit. I told him to shave it off.'

'I thought you said he had blond hair and glasses.'

'How dare you. Bobbies in my day wouldn't have answered back like that. Are you saying I don't know what my own nephew looks like? I've got a good mind to write to your boss and tell him how rude you've been.'

Collins had heard enough of this nonsense and drove on without answering.

'Just look at that,' she said as they drove along. 'That used to be a fishmonger's, and that next to it used to be a baker's, and see this art gallery thingy here, it used to be an ironmonger's. Now look at 'em. All trendy shops selling stuff they like to call retro and shabby-chic, whatever that's supposed to mean. That's not retro. Bring back the fishmongers and the ironmongers – that's proper retro.'

Collins was inclined to agree, but didn't want to enter into the conversation. The mobile rang again and he could see it was Radford trying to call him.

A few minutes later he pulled up by the beach huts near the quay. In the distance a small crowd had gathered down by the shoreline. Why is it that small crowds always seem to have gathered by the time he arrived on the scene? Why was that? He could see Radford running up the beach towards him holding onto his cap, waving his arms in the air. Collins turned to the old lady. 'This is where you get out, Madam, I'm afraid. I've got to go down to the beach, there's been an incident.'

'Ooo, has someone been murdered?'

'I don't know.'

'Maybe it's the ghost of Peter Cushing come back as Dracula and he's sunk his sharp fangs into a local virgin and left her on the beach for the vultures.'

'Yes, maybe, Madam. Actually, no, Peter Cushing never played Dracula, that was Christopher Lee.'

'Maybe it's a huge cruise liner that's come adrift on the

shore?'

Collins looked out across the beach. 'I think we'd be able to see it, don't you, Madam?'

'Well maybe it's a giant oyster that's lurched out of the waves and swallowed a dog? Maybe it's Crabzilla, that big horrible crab people keep saying lurks in the deep, dark, murky, fathomless, inky depths of Whitstable Bay?'

Collins was losing his patience. 'It's not that deep, Madam. Look, I need to get on, would you mind getting out?'

She opened the door and heaved herself up. 'I don't know why we pay our taxes if this is the service we receive from the Bobbies these days, I really don't, and me – an invalid!' She slammed the door and tutted to herself.

'Thank God you're here, Sir,' said Radford, panting to catch his breath.

'Lead the way, Radford, let's see what all the fuss is about.'

The old lady turned around. 'Simon? Is that you, Simon?'

'Aunty Jean! What are you doing here?'

Collins mouth dropped open in disbelief.

'This lady… is your Aunty, Radford?'

'I've left me zimmer frame at Morrison's, Simon, we must go and get it.'

Radford held her by the hand. 'Of course, Aunty Jean, but can we just wait a while? Something's been washed up by the waves and I've got to see what Inspector Collins thinks about it.'

The three of them walked across the pebbles down towards the shore. As they approached they could see people with mobiles in their hands taking photos. Collins pushed his way through the crowd. 'Stand back. Stand back please.'

Lying on the sand was a dead budgerigar. It was large blue one with beautiful black and white markings across its back and across the tips of its wings. Its beak was a deep golden-yellow and had a benign smile; such a gentle looking creature, but it was certainly dead. Its eyes were half-closed and its curled claws stuck up in the air like large fish hooks. Collins walked slowly around the carcass as the crowd looked on in silence. By his reckoning it was eleven, maybe twelve feet in length.

Radford knelt down and pulled loose strands of seaweed from its body. He placed his hand on the poor bird's head and gently stroked its wet feathers. He looked up at Inspector Collins.

'Sir, look,' said Radford, pointing to the bird's neck. 'Two large puncture marks.'

'It's a vampire! It's a vampire!' screamed the old lady. 'Peter Cushing has come back! Peter Cushing has come back as a vampire to save us all from this plague! A plague of locusts and mice and praying mantises eating my knickers that I only bought brand new last week from Marks and Spencer's, a plague sent to Whitstable to punish everyone for their debauchery and evil ways and opening them trendy shops and now he's back, Peter Cushing has come back to save us all!'

'Well Sir..?' said Radford, with trepidation in his voice. '... what do you think?'

Collins sighed and plunged his hands deep into in his trouser pockets. He walked around the huge body of the dead bird once more; the crowd moved back a little as he did so. He did this several times and finally came to a stop. He breathed in sharply through his bottom teeth and shook his head slowly from side to side.

'Sir?' said Radford again, looking up at his boss, eagerly waiting for his assessment of the situation. 'Sir, what do you think?'

Collins shook his head again. 'Well, I've seen a lot of budgies in my time, Radford, but this is certainly the biggest.'

Oysters without Pearls

by Joanne Bartley

The random Christmas present my brother told me was some new kind of rubber…Whizzing to the edge of the cul de sac on my bike… The two fused for my big idea, a light bulb moment on a grey day.

Our town needed this plan.

When we'd moved to Whitstable we stared with wonder at the sea; every pebble on the beach seemed interesting and different.

'Look at this, Mummy!'

A month later we looked for oyster shells and didn't see the pebbles. Pebbles were the same, pebbles everywhere. The shells scattered here and there were our treasures.

For a little while.

'Can we look at the boats now?'

Sometimes we threw pebbles into the sea. Splash, splash, splash. We were trying to put the beach back where it belonged.

'Can we go home now, Mummy?'

I didn't want to go home, but we couldn't stay. If every family threw pebbles in the sea, how long would it take until the beach was gone? Would anybody miss it?

The tourists would arrive and gawp at the hole where the beach had been.

'We put the beach back. Sorry, we didn't want it anymore.'

When we moved here the children ran to the beach. A

month later I persuaded them with scooters and bikes. Six months later it was offers of ice cream.

'Can I have a lolly too?'

I kicked an oyster shell and it scattered towards a pile of dry seaweed. There were oysters here, but there were never any pearls. Whitstable was famous for oysters, oysters were famous for pearls, but every shell was empty.

Whitstable's treasure was never the oyster's cold salty flesh. It needed sour lemon to make it taste of anything. You had to throw it down your neck without thinking, then you'd laugh and pull a face. My friends would say how marvellous our town was and I'd smile a lie back. We wouldn't talk until their next weekend visit.

It was no good complaining about a problem; if you found a problem you should fix it. So that's why I decided to use my rubber putty and play a game.

I would add pearls to Whitstable oysters. I would make a Whitstable treasure hunt.

'This is boring, Mum.'

I was staring at the sea. 'Yes, I suppose it is. Let's go home.'

The rubber was some innovative new substance. It stuck anything to anything. It was waterproof, heatproof, dish-washer proof... but was it Whitstable proof?

I fanned out the tiny silver packets. I noticed each was decorated with a coloured dot. Red dots, yellow dots, pink, blue, and green. I picked up the green packet. Green for go.

I spent the next three days working out the plan. A hidden object would reveal the name of a Whitstable road. If you went to that road and looked you would find another clue. Each clue led to another road, each road had a hidden clue, each clue led to another road, and another...

There were lots of interesting Whitstable road names.

'I'm seeing an osteopath on Oxford Street.'

'You need to go all the way to London?'

'No. Oxford Street. Here.'

The memory made me cringe. But mostly the road names

were good.

'Right, you two, scooter or bike?'

Just sulks.

'Ice cream?'

Not hungry.

'Coffee ice cream?'

I'd once offered them coffee ice cream at Sundae Sundae and the caffeinated treat had tempted them.

Anything to bully them out of the house. I wanted to go to satisfy some inner demon, but I understood their lack of interest in the world outside their front door.

Beautiful things lose their beauty over time; your eyes need surprise. The newness of things seems to open them wide. Every rainbow makes us look to the sky.

My first clue was a Lego man. Such a silly little thing. I'd picked the hat and tool carefully to fit the road name. I had no idea if this first clue was too obvious or too obscure. I started my game on Diamond Road. There was no Pearl Road so a diamond was the next best thing.

I still wanted a pearl.

Every day we passed the new housing block when we walked to school. The windows were strange because they had patio doors leading nowhere, there was no balcony outside only fresh air. You could turn the handles and go inside – but only if you could fly.

A lady walked by and muttered, 'Eyesore.'

'Really?' I looked again.

'Shouldn't have been allowed.'

She was right, it was not a pretty building. But modern houses were rarely attractive.

My children loved seeing this building grow from rubble, to scaffolding, to homes. We joked about putting trampolines under the windows so people could use their funny-window doors. We wondered if they could bounce high enough to get back in.

Isn't curiosity beautiful?

The road names were an important part of my plan. Whitstable was famous for its alleys. Squeeze Gut Alley was named after a fat policeman who couldn't squeeze through the lane as he chased children. Cuckoo Down Lane must once have once had a cuckoo falling down.

I took my green putty from the pack and stuck a Lego man to the back of a lamp post.

'What are you doing, Mum?'

Was this graffiti? I wondered if this was setting a bad example to my children. But my Lego man could only be found by someone who looked carefully. I had many more clues in my bag. They might have looked like junk but they weren't.

I bent down and tugged the bow on my shoe. 'Just tying my shoe lace.'

The next road was a place I'd never been before; the name had caught my eye. The Lego man led here if his clue was solved.

I unwrapped my rubber, red this time. The clue was a broken plate.

'Why are we here, Mummy?'

'I don't know. I've never been here before.'

It was starting to drizzle and I thought of going home. It was an ordinary road but I noticed a giant sunflower in a pot.

'Look at that!' It was taller than a front door and the flower was bright yellow. Polly stared at the picture book flower. I took my opportunity and stuck a clue to a gate post.

I was adding surprise to Whitstable's streets. The children didn't understand the significance, but I jollied them along.

'Not another road,' Luke groaned.

I felt bad dragging them to so many random places. I thought of going home but then I noticed the sky.

'A rainbow!'

We looked up to the sky. I took my opportunity and hid a clue beside a tree.

A week later we played the game for the first time.

'What does this mean?' The children crouched to decipher a

clue under a bench. I loved their anticipation, the way excitement made their words tumble out.

'I don't know what it all means,' I smiled. It was true.

'This is fun, Mum.' Luke prodded the clue.

'I've got it!' Polly yelled.

'I want the map.' Luke snatched my printed google map. 'Don't worry, I'll work it out.'

Next weekend it was, 'Can we do the treasure hunt again?'

They hadn't reached the end yet, which was good, there wasn't any end.

'Of course!' I enjoyed being the secret fun giver.

After school we played again. We visited the Lego man, the broken china, the bench and the rest.

'Can we take Dad?' the children asked next time.

I didn't think my husband would be a treasure hunt fan, and I was right. He deliberated over the Lego, then gave up and made the children tell him the answers.

'Can we do that treasure hunt again?' Polly asked a few days later when she got home from nursery.

'Of course!' I told her.

The miracle rubber was still on the lamp post, the Lego man was still wearing his hat... They always gave up after five clues, but they never seemed to mind, they were ready to come home.

When the children went to bed I decided to stick more clues. I said we needed bread and my husband barely noticed.

A few days later and we hit a weekend without plans. 'We've got to get the kids out of the house,' he said.

I wanted to suggest my treasure hunt, but thought everyone must be fed up of it by now.

'Let's do the treasure hunt!' Luke yelled. 'You are a good clue solver, Dad.'

'I want to stay home,' Polly said.

'You can bring your bike,' I said.

We persuaded the children to put on their coats, we said they'd be home soon.

The frost turned our breath to clouds. Everyone groaned when I suggested visiting the Horsebridge, it seemed I was the only one interested in art with a theme of regrowth.

'Aren't we doing the treasure hunt?' Luke asked.

'A toy stuck to a lamp post on some random street?'

My husband was grumpy. We would go home to our cosy prison. No visitors wanted oysters, it was just the four of us for months.

'I'll take you to George's to buy a toy, you've got your pocket money.'

We visited George's, then the library next.

My husband watched a TV repeat, I went out in the dark and hid more clues.

'Should we do the treasure hunt again?' I asked the next weekend.

'I'm playing,' Luke said.

'We can get an ice cream.'

He didn't look up from the game.

'Coffee flavour?'

I went out on my own. I said we needed milk but the truth was I couldn't face being home. My family wouldn't miss me; I would return before my mum-guilt kicked in.

The weather was fine. It was a rare February with no ice-wind.

The people of Whitstable were pursuing their ordinary missions, dull secrets that mattered only to them. They were the pebbles on the beach, too many to count. The newcomers were different, blue hair, a vintage dress, a sparkle in the eye. They were my oyster shells.

But still no pearls.

In my pocket I carried more clues and packets of rubber stuff. My bag was full of junk connected to street names. But I didn't want to hide any more clues. I was giving up. What was it all for? I would stick them, and stick them, but no one ever found them, no one even knew they were there.

Just a silly game.

I was annoyed by a town that promised too much, by my naivety that life was always sunny by the seaside, by my restlessness and lack of commitment. Yes, I would give up my treasure hunt. It was a hunt with no end. There was no treasure.

'I don't even know how pearls are made,' I said to my husband when I got home.

He laughed. 'You're hopeless, you were such an embarrassment on the quiz team.'

He explained oyster science. A grain of sand irritated the oyster flesh, it coated it… Not sure how… The oyster wanted the substance to go away, but it would only layer it with layer after layer of… I don't know what.

Yes, I am bad at quizzes. I know that. I don't know what the oyster did, or how it did it, or why. I don't know, and maybe he is right and I'm stupid. Somehow a speck of sand is transformed into a gem.

I hate this town. We'd get a bigger house in Herne Bay. Margate is improving. I always liked Broadstairs and we all loved Morelli's ice cream. Maybe we should move? Maybe I should? Me and the kids.

I walked down Nelson Road towards the beach. At Windy Corner Stores the usual crowd sat, with woolly scarves and soya milk lattes.

I walked past the tennis courts to the beach, I sat on a wall staring at the sea. I didn't throw pebbles. I didn't look for the oyster shells.

The penguins painted on the groyne were faded, the sea had washed the picture away. Most people seemed okay with Catman painting where he pleased. I always thought he had a cheek.

No one knew about my Whitstable game, but I reached into my handbag and found a notebook and pen. I wrote my messages:

Look up at the owl.

The first is on Diamond Road.

Under the bench at the station.

Try the railing by the Oval.

At the Neptune round the back.

My sticky rubber gift led me to this moment; a little boy whizzed past on a bike and I remembered that feeling. I smiled. I had my mission. I would play.

I placed a note on the table at Windy Corner. A bearded man put his fork down, he noticed.

I stuck a note to the side of the bus stop. An old lady paused to read what it said.

More in the library, between the pages of some books. I stuck one on the community noticeboard in Costa Coffee, then put one on a table at the Black Dog.

I kept writing and sticking, and scattering my notes. This was my treasure hunt, people might ignore it, or not get the notes, but some might want to play.

I saw someone put a note in their pocket. I saw two children run in the direction of Diamond Road.

I saw people curious and fun-loving. I saw people having a go.

Why not? I'd had a go too, why the hell shouldn't I?

I knew what I would do.

I lifted the lid of my jewellery box. I took out my necklace. The necklace I'd worn on my wedding day. My husband had wound it and wound it around my neck, but now I would be free of its constraints.

I snipped the string with some scissors; the pearls slid on to the bed. Pretty litter on the duvet cover of our marriage bed. I started to gather them up.

'What are you doing?'

He could still be appeased if I lied. I still had a chance. I could tell him my necklace had broken.

'I have a prize for my treasure hunt. It needs a prize.'

I was scared, but he only snarled. 'You're such a child.'

I carried my pearls right past him, two handfuls of treasure. He didn't stop me. I couldn't explain why I did it. It just felt right. I hid my tiny gems. They were the final prize, in case my clues were ever solved.

Victory.

Was this a victory?

I didn't know whether to be happy or sad. It was the end of something. Newness is good.

The children didn't mention the treasure hunt again; perhaps they connected it to living with their dad. I would notice families looking at the groynes and wonder if they might have found a clue. Were my clues still there? I didn't know how long miracle rubber stuck things together, or whether it was Whitstable proof.

Luke was splashing in the sea, his sister shivered, laughed, and splashed back. I picked up a pebble. It was smooth and grey, if you looked at it closely you could see dots of many different shades. It was beautiful.

I ran into the sea to be with my children. The water-shock was good. The excitement made me want to giggle. The sea was different every time. Icy or cold, clear or muddy, seaweed or just stones, grey-brown or blue-grey, sharp or not sharp – if you remembered your beach shoes. Sometimes we would stay until the evening then look at the sunsets, pink or purple or orange, a new surprise in the sky every day.

Pearls are made from layers. I think about that sometimes. The oysters turn an ordinary thing into treasure. I had found my treasure, the clues led me here. My treasure was all around, it was everywhere. You just had to open your eyes and see it.

The Magician

By Lin White

My baby brother loved magic.

By the age of six, he could already do several tricks. His favourite pastime was entertaining friends and family. And he was good. I mean really good. His card tricks were amazing, he could make things appear out of nowhere and he was working his way through new tricks as fast as he could learn them. I was five years older, and I couldn't work out how he did it. Any attempt I made ended in failure.

His hero was a guy simply called The Magician, and he was desperate to go and see him perform. He would talk of little else.

But he also loved the sea, and boats. So we often used to go to the harbour and watch the boats. There were the fishing boats, the lifeboat, and sometimes a visiting steamship would provide even more excitement.

It was one sunny June afternoon that it happened. We'd gone to the harbour after school, waiting for the steamship to arrive and disembark all the passengers who had sailed over from Southend. I was never sure afterwards how it had happened – had he been leaning over, or had he slipped on something, or just lost his balance? I guess we'll never know.

But he fell into the harbour.

I didn't even notice. I'm his big sister. I was supposed to be looking after him, and when he fell in the harbour I didn't even know.

Luckily one of the fishermen was in his boat in the harbour, sorting out his nets. He let out a massive shout, which made me turn and look. The moment I realised Kyle wasn't in sight my heart stopped.

I ran to the edge of the harbour and looked down into the water, where the man had thrown a lifebelt and was frantically stripping off his boots and jersey. He jumped into the water, and another man who was in the harbour climbed down the ladder and started swimming as well.

There were several moments of shouting and screaming and splashing, and then the two men between them carried my brother's limp, lifeless body up the ladder and laid him out on the quay, where a crowd of tourists and locals and holiday-makers had gathered.

One of the women there knew first aid, and she started pumping on his chest. She and others took it in turns to work on him, while I stared on in horror. It seemed like several lifetimes until the ambulance turned up, siren blaring, and the paramedics loaded him in the ambulance and took him off. The woman who had kept him alive took me home, and explained to Mum what had happened, because I found I couldn't speak.

I've never spoken since. It's as though he stole my voice. The doctors said it was the shock, and that I'd talk again when I was ready, but five years on I was still silent.

On the day Kyle nearly drowned, Mum and I got in the car and drove to the office where Dad worked. He jumped in, his face white, and we drove through to Ashford Hospital, where Mum rushed up to the desk in the Emergency Department and yelled at the poor woman on duty.

Kyle was still alive. At first that was all we needed to know, but gradually the truth became clear. He would never be the same again.

He had broken a leg when he fell, and he had been starved of oxygen, causing brain damage. His leg healed okay, but his brain didn't. 'He's young, and the brain is flexible at that age,' they all told us. 'He'll recover.'

And then, 'He's still young. There's no telling what he will be able to do. The brain is remarkable.'

And then, 'We just don't know. There have been cases… you just need to be patient.'

And then they stopped saying anything about him.

Mum went on caring for him, Dad went on burying himself in his work and I silently went on with my life as best I could, and through it all, little Kyle would sit in his specially adapted wheelchair, which supported his head and stopped his legs from moving around, and he would watch the world around him with a blank expression on his face, until we almost forgot about the lively little boy he once was. It was like he was the family pet; we'd make such efforts to include him in events and outings, and he never showed any indication that he was even aware of who we were, let alone what was happening around him.

And then we met him. The Magician.

He claimed to be able to do magic. Not tricks, but actual magic. No one believed him, of course; they all tried to spot the trick. To work out how it was done. To debunk his work.

Videos were made and pored over frame by frame. Photos were taken, enlarged and scrutinised. People would stand and watch closely. Never was a hint seen of how his tricks were achieved.

At first, they considered it a joke. There must be a trick, so he must just be very good at hiding it. But as time went on and no one worked it out, tempers flared. He was the subject of several hatchet attacks in the press, calling him a fraud, but there was never any proof.

And still, he took no notice. He calmly told people that he could do magic, denied there was any trick and refused to elaborate.

Then one day he walked into our lives and changed them forever.

He was going to perform at Whitstable Playhouse; an odd choice for such a famous magician, but then he seemed to choose his shows on a whim, one week performing at a big city theatre with a thousand in the audience, and then the next week in a small theatre in an obscure town somewhere, usually near the sea.

When we heard he was coming to Whitstable, my father insisted that we should go, and take Kyle. Mum hated the idea. I said nothing, of course. But Dad insisted. He spoke to the theatre, who made special arrangements to fit his wheelchair in. Mum just cried. I think she always felt guilty that she had let us go to the harbour on our own, that somehow his failure to recover was her fault. Dad never said anything to her about it, but I think he blamed her too. Kyle was his precious son, his darling, and it was almost as though he didn't notice how he was these days; he still behaved as though Kyle was sleeping, or slacking, and seemed convinced that one day he would just get up and walk away from the wheelchair as though the last five years had been a dream.

Me? I watched my parents' pain in silence, unable to speak even to ease their suffering, feeling that if only I'd been watching him more closely, then nothing would have happened to him, and, by extension, to me.

So there we were, the broken family, grief-stricken mother, angry father, dumb daughter and vegetable son, sitting in the front row of the theatre, waiting for the show to start. The theatre was packed. I heard murmurs from the people directly behind us; my father is a tall man, and my brother in his wheelchair was not small.

The magician stepped out onto the stage and all fell silent. Watching, waiting. It was all we had imagined and more. He started small, with simple tricks that any magician could do. Then he built up to bigger tricks, wilder tricks, tricks that brought gasp after gasp from the audience. Even Kyle seemed to be watching him intently.

Most people barely noticed when it happened. He stopped,

stared down into the audience and said, 'I need a volunteer.' Nearly everyone started waving their hands in the air, of course. Everyone except my family. But he seemed to focus in on us, and pointed. 'Yes, you, please. Come up to the stage and say hello.'

I started to shake my head. But it wasn't me he was pointing at. It was Kyle. And Kyle was fumbling clumsily with the buckles and straps that held him into his wheelchair and standing up and stumbling, then walking – no, running – up the steps to the stage, to applause from the audience.

Most of them thought nothing of it, of course. But those around us, who had seen him get out of the wheelchair, thought it was a set-up. That all our arguments about giving a treat to the poor disabled child were a scam to get seats, while depriving other people of their chance to see the show from such a good position.

We knew different. We sat, staring in awe, as Kyle introduced himself and chatted happily with the Magician.

It was a simple trick – Kyle walked up a couple of steps, through a door, and reappeared at the back of the theatre through another door. Most people were in awe at the speed of the trick – we couldn't see through the door because of the angle, but it was just as though we were seeing the other side of the door at the back, that the door he went in through and the door he came out from was the same door, although they were separated by a few hundred feet and a couple of hundred people.

We were in awe of the fact that it was Kyle up there, walking and talking and seeming perfectly normal.

He waved to everyone from the back of the theatre, picked out by the spotlight, walked calmly back to his seat past the audience, and joined us in the front row. He hesitated for a minute, looking at his wheelchair. I silently stood, let him sit in my seat, and then sat on the floor in front of him. That's how we stayed until the end of the show.

We let everyone else leave first, ignoring the angry mutters from those close to us, until there was just the four of us sitting there; Dad, stern and upright. Mother, her face in her hands, silently weeping. Me, sitting on the floor staring blankly up at the empty stage. And Kyle, sitting in the theatre seat looking round as though wondering what we were doing there.

The manager was furious. He seemed to think that Kyle had been faking it. I listened to him speaking to my parents afterwards, in that quiet, angry tone that's on the verge of shouting. Talking about how manipulative it was, how unfair to deceive others, how he should prosecute them for fraud. My parents just kept staring at Kyle, and barely said a word. In the end, I'd had enough.

'You just don't understand,' I told him. 'Leave us alone.' And I turned and walked away, pushing the wheelchair, leaving the rest of my family to follow me open-mouthed, and trying to understand how I could suddenly speak again.

So, was it all a con? Did my little brother spend five years pretending to be disabled in order to pull off an incredible magic trick? Or did The Magician really heal him, and release the grip around my throat?

I tried to contact The Magician, but he disappeared from public sight, and as far as I know, no one knows where he went. But I found that in the last few performances he had put on, there had been some sort of miracle taking place relating to someone in the audience.

I guess with us, he got two for the price of one.

In the Company of Oysters

by John Wilkins

I smashed up my guitar and never played it again for ten years after I found out what happened. Maureen never worked again behind the bar in the Duke of Cumberland after that New Year's Eve. She was the principal attraction at the Duke of Cumberland, whoever was playing there. I suspected it was Maureen who was the writer identified by the initial 'M', at the end of the *In Memoriam* notice dedicated to Patrick. The notice appeared every year, in the last edition of the Whitstable Times published before New Year's Eve.

I had never been able to read it all the way through. So I have written down my part in his last night. It's my *In Memoriam*, what follows. To move on, I want try to explain to the family how it happened; then perhaps, as the counsellors have all advised, I can accept that I will always be unforgiven...

The family haven't spoken to me since Patrick's funeral. At least or more honestly *at last* I have tried to explain the events of New Year's Eve to myself by remembering what I can. I can remember one fact – nobody knew how quickly the tide would come in.

After all, it was me who made the bet with Patrick about the *unobtainable* – I was the one who came up with the idea in the first place. I suggested to Patrick that we have a bet that he couldn't seduce Maureen, whom I had always believed to be unobtainable...

Maureen was the sister of a friend of mine, Mike. He was the lead guitarist of the trio I played electric bass for, on that New Year's Eve in the Duke of Cumberland. I wondered if it was worth tracking her down, to find out why, even after all these years, she still wanted us to be reminded that she was sorry. At least then I would know for certain that it was she who reminded us every year. I don't really know everything about what happened between her and Patrick on that New Year's Eve.

Maureen had all the attributes that made a barmaid very popular, yes all of them. She also had a look that she gave you as you entered the bar; as if she had been watching out for you, and at last you had arrived. She made you feel that you were the only one in the bar that night that she was really interested in. A swift dip of the head from her gave you quite an acknowledgement, and there was a chance of what Maureen might offer later. You would just have to wait and see, have more to drink, while you waited to see where all this was leading to, with her. If you managed to hang around until last orders, then it could be *your* night, she made you believe. Maureen could bewitch you like that. Bewitched, you always thought Maureen wanted you.

There was a legend at the time, that she had a weakness. If you could find out what it was then you would finally unleash the passion in her. It was the mystery in her green eyes, bright and fresh as the salt spray of the sea, ten minutes away from where you stand with a drink in the bar of the Duke, as the locals called it. The weakness could only be exposed in sight of the sea by the oyster beds. Just a short walk away from the Duke. It wasn't a complicated route, just crossing over the high street, into Terry's Lane and up to the Keam's Yard car park, straight across it, then up the few steps onto the walkway. It felt as if you were presenting yourself to the court of King Neptune when you stood on it, above the beds looking out to sea.

Everyone saw it in the papers, everyone who was in the Duke on that New Year's Eve remembered Maureen and who she went with.

'Yes, I remember Patrick – he was the one who they found by the oyster beds. It was a dog walker in the morning. The dog had wandered over to the head and started barking, only the head was visible by the oyster bed.' He was the youngest suitor to have taken her down to the oyster bed, although they never made it further, I discovered later. They never found out exactly how it happened. No one knew who buried him there up to his neck. It couldn't be proved one way or the other if they knew the tides would turn and drown him where he was buried, up to the neck. The old salts who hung about the RNLI shop explained to everyone who asked that the tide came in quicker for all sorts of reasons, a high wind was just one contributory factor. If a high wind combined with other changes then the tide would rise faster – you couldn't always predict it with complete accuracy, they said to the investigating police officers at the time.

The last person known to see him alive was Maureen; she had looked back after she walked away. She heard all the shouting and laughing, when the others left him. She thought she could hear Patrick laughing and enjoying the joke, that's what she said.

There had been many suitors for Maureen in the Duke, all unsuccessful until that New Year's Eve. Maybe the spark was never there, or the spell could not be cast – everyone was given just one chance and when Maureen gave them her rebuttal, they accepted it. If anyone had been successful in seducing her then Maureen must have bought their silence somehow. Nobody bragged of such a conquest in the Duke, ever.

The rejected felt just that; even asking for another chance would be pointless. What was worse, they might have to face Maureen ignoring them when they visited the Duke in future. It was thought that Maureen might not always be able to look after herself and one or two took a quiet stroll behind her along the oyster bed when she walked down there with her choice (until they were certain that they had seen Maureen return safely back to Whitstable, down Beach street into Harbour street where she rented a flat over an art gallery there). They almost believed that their vigilance might win them a second chance, one night. This is how it was with Maureen – her admirers never really gave up on her. They continued to use the Duke, all the while watching wistfully, in case that glance came their way again, offering the slimmest hope of another chance. Some of the rejected left – they had given it their best shot and accepted their rejection as final. They tried to find somewhere or someone else to pursue, that might offer a better hope of some sort of success.

On that New Year's Eve there was a busy, bubbling, foaming, boozy night going on. It was a bouncing energy dancing in the Duke. The way the drinkers danced seemed as if they were syncopated to the dark primeval blues of our trio that stretched and contracted the minutes and the moments behind and in front of the bar. It was as if the energy added to the alcohol strength of the beer drunk in the Duke that night. Then halfway through the band's first set (we called ourselves *Flavour* – we were an easily acquired taste for the clientele, who were by no means averse to a shot of twelve bar rhythm and blues), a bunch of lads squeezed in, tumbled through the doors, as if pulled in by our music that echoed and vibrated out into the night. Their leader was Patrick; his energy and disarming smile helped them to make their way to the bar, where the landlord promptly asked for, and was given, identification that proved that they were old enough to be served; and if they caused anyone any grief, then no blame could be laid at the landlord's door for encouraging underage drinkers to light a fuse on a sparkling New Year's Eve in the Duke.

Patrick's hand held a twenty pound note visibly above the heads of those drinking at the bar. As he rested his elbow on the bar he leant over it further, to stake his claim to be served next. Maureen looked along and caught the eye of the landlord, who nodded his assent to everyone behind the bar, that Patrick and his friends could be served. The landlord was the ultimate authority in this world. Then Maureen looked back down the bar at the boy and saw him looking at her. It was a look that held her attention more than any other had that evening. She felt his appreciative appraisal of her as he told her what drinks he wanted. When she placed the first full glass on the bar in front of him, there was a slight pause as their gaze locked, before he repeated the rest of his order to her. Maureen blinked as if to break his spell and was able to fill another glass. That connection was there each time that she served Patrick or one of his friends for the rest of the night.

Finally it was midnight and the stomping goodbye from the band finally lifted the roof off the Duke. The landlord roared his unwelcome command and last orders were served.

Patrick caught Maureen's eye as she put down the last full glass she was allowed to pour. A raucous countdown began to mark the start of the New Year. She could lip-read what he said – it had been said to her many times, but she nodded back her consent. She opened and closed her fists to him twice meaning she would meet him outside in twenty minutes. Maureen knew how long it took for her to finish what was expected of her behind the bar. Patrick's friends moved on to celebrate the New Year, leaving the Duke of Cumberland behind them, with one or two sly winks at Patrick, wishing him good luck.

Patrick looked flushed, from where I stood packing up our kit at the top end of the bar. His imagination fermented, as he recalled how many offers Maureen had declined that night. The rest had been firmly refused with a definite shake of the head, and occasionally he caught her shouting 'No Way!' finishing with peals of laughter to declare the matter closed.

Patrick waited outside the Duke's front doors and it seemed as if every cheer welcoming in the New Year was echoing in the street, until Maureen appeared. She came through the doors surrounded by admirers but she turned away from them. Maureen moved her head, looking up and down until she saw Patrick. With the wave of her hand to him, she seemed almost to breeze across the high street into Terry's Lane. Maureen gave the slightest of nod of her head so that Patrick understood in which direction to follow her as the crowd outside the Duke milled about in drunken embraces and slow motion stagger.

As I came through the doors carrying an amplifier, I could see Patrick and her quickly walking up the lane, ahead of those planning to continue the party on the beach. A girl I had fancied for a long time invited me to join the party and I accepted. Among the crowd was Mike, the lead guitarist, who appeared to have brought a crate of wine from a secret source to help us enjoy the night even more.

Maureen and Patrick had reached the beach and were sitting down beyond the sea wall, in front of the oyster bed, by the time we passed them. All we could hear was Maureen's laughing – Patrick was obviously entertaining her, in a way that she was enjoying. We found a spot nearer to the sea wall and footpath. We all sat around and I played guitar while the booze was handed out. For a while a few sang along, while Mike and I played guitars and managed to stumble through tunes we were still confident we could manage, in the dark. The girl who invited me whispered a request in my ear, and I turned to check what she had asked me to play, when a piercing scream stopped all of us instantly.

It sounded like Maureen – some of our group stood up, and reacting to the scream as a cry for help, ran over to where they thought the scream had come from. Soon there was more noise and some shouting and then laughter. It sounded as if there was another party starting over there. I remember thinking everything must be okay, and gradually some of them returned, but by this time, I was beginning to play only one tune for just one person to enjoy. A while later I thought I heard a voice from where the scream came from, but it was late by then and a wind had got up. The girl was taking me home – the next day, after I found out, I guessed it might have been Patrick calling for help.

I remember that while the shouting and laughing was going on, Maureen came past us, holding her throat, walking down by the sea wall on the pathway in the direction of the Beach Café past the back of the gym. I thought the way she was walking that fast just meant she wanted to go home on her own. I thought she'd had enough. I started to strum quietly the tune I had been asked to play – I was drunk enough to think I wasn't, and started playing the chords to the tune by Bob Dylan, '*Don't think twice it's alright*'. Yes, that is what the girl had asked me to play.

People had returned from the beach by then and somebody laughed – just one laugh – if I only I could recognise who had laughed then... I was told by someone whispering in my ear while I played – 'Maureen's all right and don't think twice about him – he's been taught a lesson.' It was a male voice, not the girl. I think that's what I heard, but there were a few joining in the chorus of the song and a bottle of wine was passed over to me. After taking a deep draught I continued. As the wind began to get up, I decided to finish the tune and persuade the girl it was time to go. I didn't remember my earlier promise to myself to go back and see if it was Patrick shouting. I thought it was probably just my imagination. I went back with the girl and stayed the night with her.

In the morning while the girl and I slept, a dog walker discovered the body buried in front of the oyster bed, drowned by the morning tide, only the head visible above the pebbles on the beach. When the tide receded enough, the police cordoned off the area. We were all questioned – the band, and everyone who could be identified. Maureen would not say what had caused her to scream – only that she left Patrick and the others shouting at each other on the beach. She said nothing was going on – all she wanted to do was go home to sleep.

She made some attempt to pick out people from identity parades set up by the police but she could not conclusively prove to them whether they were the people that buried Patrick up to his neck just in front of the oyster bed. She claimed that she wasn't there when they did the digging. I never knew if my brother Patrick really won the bet before he was buried in the oyster bed...

Oh Holy Night

By AJ Ivory

It's a solitary life, that of an author. One that can be passed comfortably with little public distraction.

Ordinary folk have no interest in the everyday habitudes of a writer who, for the most part, can pass unnoticed in corner shops, tea rooms, newsagents and delis. Writers have the luxury of growing into whichever form nature intended, perhaps as ugly as toads, absenting themselves from cordial workplace formalities, and small-talk niceties. They can hide themselves, observing the absurdities of human behaviour, detached as scientists peering down the lens of a microscope.

It was with these thoughts in mind that Sebastian, a retired barrister, moved to Whitstable, fixed on practising a new trade in which he would immerse himself, drawing on years of experience, penning dramas that would cast John Mortimer to shadows.

A once handsome young man, his sinewy body had succumbed to time's ravages, hours stooped over paperwork with an ink pen, birdlike eyes searching for clues on which he would build an argument, and wilt the defences of his opponent until they stood quivering like an insect caught in a jar.

Most humans were predictable, largely unintelligent and chaotic. As time passed he found their company increasingly laborious. His eighteenth century cottage was an escape, small by his standards with three double bedrooms and a study. There was a reasonable garden and a pathway fashioned from flint, which led past overgrown aloes and succulents to the front door, a period piece with wrought iron strap hinges and a knocker in the form of a lion's head.

He had brought with him a splendid and much treasured butterfly collection, mounted and framed according to Families. Each one evocative of scenes of his former life. The Pearl-Bordered Fritillary, a floor mosaic at his villa in Tuscany. The Purple Emperor, a High Court Judge in the Queen's Bench division. The Camberwell Beauty, his graduation robe. The Adonis Blue, a turquoise pendant Eleanor had worn the day she left.

In between the splayed and colourful wings of the British Empire, of humorous, irreverent sketches of courtroom dramas purchased in Chancery Lane, the ground-breaking cases of *Carlill-v-Carbolic Smoke Ball Co*, *Donnahue-v-Stevenson*, was a photo of a baby girl, no older than a year, delicate as a Small White's wing. She was displayed in no order, as if without announcement in a world where appearance is never accidental.

He had the occasional distraction of weekend sojourners, former colleagues and legal world acquaintances. On Sunday as the sun was setting, they left him to scribble his varied ideas to paper, without much disturbance. He was furnished with an appreciative bottle of wine, they all 'loved' their stay by the sea, Sebastian's cooking, his devastatingly good peanut butter parfait served with an amusing accoutrement, intended to display both style and humour. Yet invitations to London and the Home Counties passed him by. Birthdays and great occasions were spent alone shuffling around in the kitchen with his coffee percolator, the *Times*, delivered daily, and Radio 4.

Next door was a vicarage, housing Lesly, an affable widower, and his cockerel, abandoned on the doorstep after the spring harvest festival. It roused at 5h30 a.m. and sat perched on the adjoining fence, chest protruding, neck extended and feet splayed to sadistically announce the arrival of another day in Whitstable.

Sebastian was invited to a pets' blessing service, where the townsfolk would congregate under an ancient chestnut in the churchyard, surrounded by generations of their ancestors, and thank the Lord for earthly companions, great and small. He declined, deciding instead to submerge himself in local life via other means. He was no churchgoer and had no love of beasts. While he tolerated Labradors and larger breeds, he abhorred what he considered to be senile anthropomorphism practised by provincials.

A notice board at the Horsebridge Community Centre was the source of some amusement, but equal annoyance. 'The nonsense that these people indulge in.' Psychodynamic body therapy, rebirthing, crystal healing. Sebastian had joined the Conservatives Association, and partook in a regular round of golf on the green that ran alongside the railway line, behind the beach huts. He maintained private club membership at two of London's finest establishments in Holborn and Mayfair, but if he was going to write on the quotidian happenings of the sort of folk he had once prosecuted at the Bar, he felt he ought to immerse himself in their activities. He saw himself as an observer of human behaviour, a sort of anthropologist on the field. Meditation class would serve as good a start for source material as any other.

The first thing he noticed about the teacher, Helen, was her large mouth, a braying and neighing shape with solid accompanying teeth. Whitstable was full of strange characters, misshapen souls lacking in elegance and grace, sent to entertain. Helen was seated on a beanbag. She invited the group to imagine a blue light moving upwards through the base of their navel, then the sternum, past the throat chakra and out through the third eye.

As she did, she emitted a low erotic noise. He squinted observing her mouth as it slackened to the left, and her face, long as a banana, tilted as if to follow.

Sebastian decided to ask Helen for a coffee afterwards, explaining that he had recently moved to Whitstable and only knew a few people. He hoped for some light entertainment but managed to conceal it, his face earnest. Helen folded her mat, snapped it up under her arm, a little too keenly, he thought. 'Well why not, I have a free hour. Where would you like to go?'

They found a coffee shop in Harbour Street.

She was divorced. 'They always are,' he thought.

There was no talk of meditation. 'I'll have a Chi Latte with Soya. Soya's so much better for your body. We've got it wrong on the dietary front.'

Sebastian didn't care for talk of health. He watched Helen remove her shrug, bearing her shoulders, the skeletal décolletage, and a large mole at the base of her neck. He ordered an espresso, a convenient drink for a quick exit if the need arose. Helen talked in a strident, galloping pace, volunteering fragments of her life, her start in Greenwich, travels in India, her work on a Kibbutz in Haifa, her philosophy lessons, and love of writing. She never proffered much detail on any one of these phases, but watched Sebastian carefully for some indication of interest.

It did not come.

'Poor thing. Probably spews incoherent rubbish, all about women, their sacred wombs and the uselessness of men.' He decided not share his ambitions; the revelation of his craft would only complicate matters with requests to have a quick peek. There was the additional risk of intellectual property theft, the reworking his ideas, to be published in *People's Friend*, or other water closet journals.

It was late morning, the road outside lively. A bus passed, its wheels barely avoiding the pavement where toddlers ambled, candy in fists, decked in home-made jumpers of the Steiner School variety.

She had a daughter at university.

'Do you have children?' The Chai had arrived in an earthen

mug and Helen lifted it, hooking her teeth around the rim. Sebastian's thoughts drifted.

'Children?' Helen repeated, froth on her top lip.

'I do yes, a daughter. Hannah, she's twenty-four, old enough to know better.' He laughed, fidgeting. If smoking was permitted he would have lit up, blown out at least once before continuing. 'I don't hear from her often. Usually only when she wants something.'

The child lost in mounted butterflies.

Hannah, the adult reared in decreasing text messages and angry words that clung to the walls like loam.

'We were close when she was young, it's more complicated now.'

'Oh, it often is,' said Helen not wishing to disagree, 'but you love them all the same.'

Sebastian wondered if he did. A text had arrived from Hannah only that morning before class. She was coming to Whitstable on Saturday. He knew his wallet would be prised and his conscience knocked yet again.

Helen put a reassuring hand on his. He shook his head, disarmed and exposed. 'Children.'

After a polite exchange of numbers, Sebastian made his way along the High Street stopping at a butcher's and grocer's. That night he would make shepherd's pie, Hannah's favourite, and heat it just before her arrival.

The kitchen was cold, empty. Sebastian enjoyed the solitude of his own company, his clocks all ticking and the sound of gas working its way through the piping and up to the radiators. But there were times when his mind did him no favours and this was one of them. He had not seen Hannah since her brief visit over New Year, after the skiing trip he had paid for, seven months back. He fretted over what he would say, what to avoid, how to react to what she said, to the irritants she would throw at him like wet tissue missiles hurled in boarding school dormitories.

He turned on the radio, catching the opening of a drama

by an unknown author, H. Brady. A simple tale of an Eritrean immigrant and his daughter at their first visit to a London Christmas market on 23rd December.

Oh Holy Night.

As Sebastian lifted the kitchen knife dicing carrots, he found himself standing still, waiting for the next line. Somewhere between the tinsel of market stands, the child went missing and her father ran through the carnival rides and pools of light, shouting, calling for the daughter he had rescued from their homeland, now as lost as a small golden ring in a pond.

When she was little, Sebastian would take Hannah to London markets. She loved them, Borough, Leadenhall, and Portabello Road on Sunday mornings, and he would buy her a tiny printer's tray treasure.

He had surprised himself. After dreading the thought of a mewing brat in their ordered, tidy world, a smiling girl with dimpled hands and clear milk teeth had imprinted herself somewhere in the centre of his chest, in a strange and unfamiliar place no one touched. The feeling was both wondrous and terrifying and he carried her with pride, holding her as carefully as a schoolboy carrying a fish in the water bowl of his own cupped hands.

Hannah's train arrived at 11h20 on Saturday morning. She was dressed in Uggs, dark leggings, a wrap from All Saints and a stylish wide-brimmed hat. Her hair was pulled back, displaying coppery cheek bones. Each time he saw her, Sebastian marvelled at the beauty of his daughter, so like her mother.

They greeted each other with an air kiss. She wouldn't be staying long. Enough time to glance round, humouring him on a perfunctory tour of the house, her bedroom transported from twenty years back, the childish dresser, two china cats on a lace coaster, a ballerina dancing in its pink jewellery box.

'Yeah, it's nice, Dad,' said Hannah, slouching at the oak table in the kitchen, feet up, stubbing her cigarette in an Edwardian saucer. And after a few questions, some of which she seemed to forget had already been asked, she got down to business.

She was buying a flat in Finsbury Park and needed a deposit.

If Sebastian had felt emasculated by his daughter, he had felt it more keenly with his wife.

Eleanor.

He would see her first thing in the morning in the breakfast room surrounded by orchids and light, her bare arms toned, a simple glistening bracelet, slim legs crossed, one foot looped round the back of the other. She entertained with careless elegance, coiffed and crisp in her Eskander shirts, surrounded by the Sunday supplement crowd, Veueve Cliquot business-women finalists, conscience campaigners, fashionistas. Her meals were impeccable, no endangered species, nothing controversial. No one wrestled with the dilemma of foie gras or swordfish; nor were they embarrassed by chickpeas or tofu.

It was in this thoughtfully selected company that Sebastian had drank through the cocktail and port selection, degenerating.

His infidelity started with a work placement student at Chambers and ended with the au pair. Eleanor had known it all along, silently tolerating it, never letting the ball of jealousy drop. She would choose her moment, and did. Returning from a feigned departure to Berlin she caught him, trousers down, in the nanny's comforting Estonian arms. She had her ammunition and a small child to support. It would cost Sebastian a fortune, a fair size of it on legal fees.

Hannah was buying a house at twenty-four.

Sebastian knew full well that the most reasonable question delivered with the wrong intonation, inaccurately translated, would have her bolt. Still he felt a prod of indignation, a fight in him wanting to rear up and spread its wings. 'Her mother must have put her up to this. Fleecing me again when the child maintenance has run its course.'

From what he knew, the purchase made no sense. Hannah worked sporadically as a freelance photographer sharing a basement with some bass guitarist, his Camden gigs and a silly daytime job involving IT or software. The place was tucked away in the Northern suburbs, inching off the tube line, the lifestyle sporadically propped up by Eleanor's occasional contribution when their finances sank into that low pit known as London Life.

'Well.' Sebastian stood up, pocketing his hands, fingering stray coins. 'The first time. It's a big step.'

He breathed out emphasising the word 'big' as if Hannah did not know what it meant.

'Shall we have something to eat? Talk it through?'

He spooned the pie onto her plate in steaming mounds and she shoved it round with a fork dangling from her limp wrist, elbows splayed and head bowed. He wished she would take off the bloody hat and look at him, but she slumped, her torso shaping a half circle, the bones of her spine a tidy row of pebbles, eyes raised suspiciously.

'You have an offer? Mortgage of some sort?'

'First time buyer's offer but I'm self-employed. We need a larger deposit.'

We.

One word, the double person pronoun, indicating, as he had learnt to the rhythm of a schoolmaster's tapping cane, not the singular person, but two.

He had to ask the question, if he was investing a penny. Was she...buying with someone? Who?

The fork fell hitting the side of her plate with blunt indignation. 'Dad, you know who. Seph. Who else?'

Sebastian's lips tightened. 'But you've only just met him, Hannah.'

'A year and a half ago. We've been living together for eight months, nine nearly.'

'Nearly nine,' Sebastian said with a snorting laugh. It was a cynical sound, the sort he would make in witness cross-examination. 'Of course, nine makes all the difference.'

'You've never even met him, never visited.'

'You've never invited me!'

'You wouldn't come, would you? Neasden ain't good enough for you. Some nasty little place on the Northern Line.' Her words and face gnarled in mockery, in deliberate imitation of her father, the dismissive flapping of his right hand.

He could feel himself transforming, reverting, to familiar vulpine. His daughter was completely unreasonable.

'So let's get this straight, Hannah. You don't bother inviting me to Neasden, you'd balk at me turning up unannounced, you strangle me with guilt nonetheless if I don't. You come here now, having blown me out at least a dozen times for some twat I've never heard of, some Pete or other's rave, some Letty's housewarming, or whatever, and you come, asking for offerings that will get some fellow who plays in a band's feet on the property ladder.'

For the seconds that this outpouring lasted, he enjoyed it, his earlier niceties and restraint discarded like a well-worn pantomime costume.

Hannah stood up. Squaring him, for a second the force of her presence beating down. The child in her a phantom.

He saw her, fourteen years old, squatting back on her haunches, gravel driveway underfoot, his Range Rover waiting like a predatory beast, her statement eyeliner smudged.

He shook his head, hands stretched apologetically, a tired old waiter who had spilt the soup. The thought of apology flicked through his mind. It was years overdue but he could not find the form or gesture it needed and sat pivoting in his kitchen chair like a ridiculous giant weeble. The girl had insulted him coming here asking for money like this. Still, the heavy glutinous sensation of attachment he felt for this girl–woman hung in the shaded kitchen, heavy, sickly and suffocating as incense.

'You judge me by the one mistake I've made.'

She turned, her passing question a belly blow.

'What was it Dad? Your mistake? Go on, say it.'

Sebastian raised his hands to his face, unable to reply.

'Your little lie, hitting me, or both?'

He opened his mouth, shaped in the form of an 'O'. Hannah turned, her slim, rock-chick calves transporting her down the corridor. He heard the gate swing back and slam on its hinges.

His little girl had turned into a dumpy teenager, gobby and angry, shared out by her parents. Birthdays with one, Christmas with the other, and with each passing they struggled. Boarding school was the easy option. Until the night she ran away, took the train back home in February.

He had opened the door, shirt unbuttoned, hair tousled and damp, the smell of fornication about him.

'Hannah, what in God's name. You're supposed to be at school.'

'Dad, I want to come home.'

'Dammit Hannah, you can't.' He stood, full framed in the door.

'Dad, let me in.' She faced him, her jaw indignant.

'For God's sake, Hannah. No. We've spoken about this. It's a bloody good school and I'm taking you back.'

'Why won't you let me in?'

As she barged forward he blocked her with his forearm, shoving her back, sharply closing the door, locking it. She cried from behind, pleading, imploring, wailing, with each phrase her voice rising with electrical undercurrent of adolescent fury.

Shirt now buttoned, a corduroy jacket enveloping him like the home counties gent he was, Sebastian emerged, keys in hand. The girl shoved herself with a force that winded him. His anger rose, curling smoke-like, teeth gritted tight, a man about to swat a wasp. He wrenched her, pulling her down the drive to the car and from behind the dim glass of his front room, she saw it. The outline of a woman's back twisting her arm into a shirt.

'Who's that? Dad, there's someone there. Who is it?'

'There's no one. No one.' He snapped out the keys. As his daughter pulled from him he dug his fingers tighter into her arm.

'Get off, you're hurting me.' She looked up, eyes panicked, and jerked backwards slinking on her haunches.

'I'm calling Mom. I'm calling the police, you...' He raised his hand. It wasn't deliberate, no malice aforethought as they called it at the Bar. A simple instinctive movement, communicating all she needed to know. Before she could duck, he slapped her. The girl stumbled back, catching her breath. Torn in half.

He clasped his wrist by the scruff as if to admonish and contain it, horrified at what he had done.

'She was hysterical,' he would tell a sympathetic headmistress later over a full-bodied glass of red in the drawing room.

And when he was tactfully asked if Hannah had seen someone he leaned forward, looked the Head straight in the eye and delivered the sort of beautifully crafted denial that would win him votes if he stood for an election. He reminded the Head that Hannah was a strange girl, with worrying tendencies, a mind that played tricks on her, and they would be wise to keep an eye on that.

For years he didn't see her. She returned eventually, emailing his Chambers, now a university drop-out in need of money. Forgiveness was an afterthought. He embraced her with enthusiasm. With every purchase, apologetic gift, Sebastian hoped he would find his child again, resurrect her like some genie from a bottle.

'First time buyer then.' Futile words to pass the time.

He stood in the garden, hands on his hip bones, eyes falling on the stretch of pathway. His daughter somewhere downhill, probably at the station. All around, the houses were silent, no stir of life. The vicar's cockerel padded the adjoining wall, staring at him.

He had lost her.

The phone in his pocket buzzed. A text message.

Hannah?

It was Helen. That god-awful creature was doing a reading at the community centre that night. Did he want to join her for some literary fun and laughter?

No, he bloody didn't. He would rather gouge his eyes out with a fire prod.

He returned indoors to the silence. Her dinner plate was on the table, the potato dry and cold. He scraped it in the bin, ascended to the study and poured himself a glass of port. Outside, the light faded to a dismal early evening and misty rain fell in whispers.

In the morning he would set about writing again and wait for news of his daughter. No doubt there would be an admonishing call from his ex-wife. He waited, the days passed, he flicked through newspapers, fired up the laptop hoping to write and words did not come.

By the following Friday, he was feeling perkier. A round of golf and a trip to the city had livened him, numbed the shock of Saturday and that dreaded feeling of guilt that seeped up like rotten debris from a plughole. The post had arrived that morning along with the *Whitstable Times*, which lay on the doorstep in a scattered pile. Sebastian was about to discard it with the recycling when something caught his eye, a familiar face on the cover, the long banana shape and bushy brows, the slightly crooked smile.

Helen. He lifted it closer, poised to release a grunt of mockery.

'Whitstable's own literary talent.'

'God,' thought Sebastian, 'these people have no clue.' He scanned the opening lines.

'Helen Brady has been known for some time in Whitstable with her witty stories and poetry readings. Now this local girl is causing something of a literary sensation on a national scale. Her first published story Oh Holy Night has won critical acclaim, and was read on BBC Radio 4 last Friday.'

Sebastian clutched the paper closer. It couldn't possibly... But it was. H. Brady, the author was Helen.

'It can't be,' he repeated, red faced and indignant. 'Not that stupid...'

Upstairs on his laptop he found it on iPlayer and sat listening as the reader's words brought back that same thudding sensation in a softer, unfamiliar part of him, where he kept Hannah's memory.

Outside, the vicar's cockerel crowed.

He saw his reflection in the glass mirror that hung proudly in the hallway, a sort of shrinking, balding form. He looked away, then back again, meeting his own eyes. As he did, he spoke slowly back to the image.

'Ruinous, arrogant bastard.'

That evening he sat down at his desk, took out some paper, and penned a submission.

It was the most important, and as it turned out, most forgiving of his life.

The following week she invited him to London and didn't stand him up. And in time, with effort, they would walk, a father and his adult daughter, along the seafront, past the Neptune and on to the harbour.

It was a letter of apology.

Skyline

By Alison Kenward

There is always that moment when the edge of the sky is lifted up gently to show some light. The greyness of the rest hangs obstinately ready for night. This end of the year, night-time comes quicker. But that gap in the sky is always there as a reminder that there is an opening somewhere, that life goes on, however dark it is just now.

She hasn't even got herself a dog since moving here. Everyone else seems to have one. But not her. So there is no reasonable excuse to be walking on the beach. But the pebbles show promise and the sky is suitably leaden. She can stand looking out like an ageing Lieutenant's woman and peruse the skyline where the oil tankers, crouching under the gap in the sky, lie in wait.

Once upon a time, she thinks, she could have been like Meryl Streep. Gazing out across the water, mysterious and beautiful. But not now. Now her looks have gone. No friends in France make contact. The seaside town provides her with space. She can walk for hours and still not run out of new places.

Without an animal at her heels, no one can bother her. The dog walkers are an elite group. If she buys a dog she must join them. She cannot do that for it would mean interaction. It would entail sharing history. She must not join.

She walks purposefully along the sea wall with an air of importance and a glassy stare, leaving throngs of dog owners encircling the tangled leads of their pets. The walkers loudly discuss the merits of the golf course, the local pop up restaurant and the latest Groupon offer. They stand in solid ranks around their animals, letting no one in and no one out, waiting patiently for their own turn to relate an event, an experience, a gossip. And as the stranger passes by, a lull in conversation emerges. And then a spark of recognition. She was that woman who… She was the one that… She has no name.

The stranger's gaze is fully focussed a few feet beyond the walkers. She is aware of the lull, the glint of recognition and quickens her pace. She is glad that people are talking about her. Or at least guessing about her. She isn't one of them; not even a DFL. She has moved here from abroad.

When he first suggested they move to France it was early in their relationship. The idea seemed to open up a landscape of possibility. A leeway towards the future. Her life was hum-drum; an enduring non-event that only remained that way due to her dutiful loyalty to her widowed mother to whom she was the sole companion. When she met François, she was thrust into a new world of excitement and delight. He was made of magic, glorious happiness and adventure, all rolled into one. She was, literally, swept away by him and felt a gratitude that was both overwhelming and fearful. The proposition to live in France was presented to her as the height of romantic love and she was emboldened to consider it despite the gnawing guilt of leaving her mother.

'All that sunshine, my love,' he would say. 'Do you good.'

And slowly but surely the charms of France and the vineyards and the promised romance became a reality and just a year later she said goodbye to her mother, her dwindling family and envious friends and left for a new adventure.

Her mother came into her bedroom where she was packing with the fervour of a small child. She looked at her daughter with small recognition and grave concern. Both expressions escaped her daughter, intent as she was on her Box of Delights.

'No regrets?' she said.

Her daughter paused and turned in surprise.

'Regrets?' she asked and then laughed with glee. 'I've had a few… But then again… too few to…' and she laughed louder at her mother, delighted at her own cleverness.

'No,' she answered after a while. 'No regrets. Don't worry about me.'

And her mother smiled gently but her eyes owned the concern. She told her to take great care.

And for a while it was blissful. They had spent their days doing up the tiny house they had bought and riding out into the countryside to admire the vineyards and the fields full of sunflowers. They gazed at each other in longing and love and she never could remember a time of such enduring bliss.

The troubled look on her mother's face came back to haunt her in the years to come for it soon became apparent that this man was a bully. There were small changes at first; a smack here, a hand on her throat there. And then the money started to run out. There had been much less than he'd promised and they argued incessantly about whose fault it was that the idyll had not been realised.

Blame ensued; she was a spendthrift, he said. She contributed nothing. She couldn't even cook properly. Then the drinking started to get heavier and he became morose. The smacks became harder, the threats more terrifying and then she knew she was trapped.

She found work in the local bar as an escape from his rages for a few hours at least. It was friendly enough but, though the customers liked her, her French was not fast enough and by the winter, the patron told her they had no need for extra help and the bar would close for two months. They had been in France for just one and a half years.

The night she came home from the bar for the last time, she knew before she had opened the door that he had gone. The quietness settled over her like a shroud. She stood still and alone and, for a moment, forgot how to breathe. Feeling left her.

148

She didn't try to find him. She knew he had gone for good. He had left in his heart long before he left in person. Time took its hold and day by day she began to place one piece of her life alongside another one.

She was alone for a long time. Or so it seemed. But she had no money for rent and had sold all his things in order to give herself time. He had left a lot that was of value.

'Take anything you want. I shan't be back for anything. Keep it or sell it. It's up to you.'

The note was brief and business-like. 'Sorry' scrawled as an afterthought.

There were some antique books and some silver and a great collection of snuff boxes, which would make another three months' worth of rent money. She knew that the antiques dealer had paid her too low a price but she gratefully took the proffered notes and stowed them away in an old handbag.

Soon she began to relax and enjoy her single status. In a way the survival was a great victory for her and she felt courage filling her up where fear had been.

There were few people she could call on for help but the village was friendly and no one asked after him, understanding that it was no business of theirs. As time went by, she turned her thoughts to England and started to plan her return.

It took another year to decide on where. She sat in the local library and poured over an old map, eventually deciding that the East Kent Coast would suit well enough. In her distant childhood she had been there once. Or was it Margate with the scary rides? She remembered a ride on a train in the summer with the seat that scratched the back of her legs. There were squashed tomato sandwiches to eat on the wind-swept beach and the distant sea ahead. There was a nervous excitement about being there on the sandy beach. She remembered the sting of it in her eyes.

So it was with some surprise that she found her memory had played her false and the beach was made up of stone. Pebbles lay at random as if thrown by a giant wind. They stared back at her as if to say, 'This is our place.' Rather like the dog walkers, they took ownership of all that lay before her. And there were no rides. This was not Margate.

The darkness is gathering with purpose now and she decides to start back. Every evening she changes the route by one alley only. They all pretty much lead in the same direction, either towards the sea or away from it, but she loves the names. Who was Reeves and who was Brice and why was one called Squeeze? Obviously it was one of the narrower ones but what about the others? Who had thought up the names? She thinks that it would be a good thing to have an alley named in her memory but knows that she is not local enough. But a memorial of some sort would be an ironic touch. For here she is faceless.

Puddles of lamplight lie on the ground; some yellow and some a grey ice. Here the journey becomes more difficult. She lives away from the centre of the town and the roads are not as well-lit as she would like. She peers ahead and can just make out her white wall on the top of the hill. Hers is a faceless cul-de-sac and the bungalow is the last one overlooking fields.

It had been a quick sale. She had rented a fisherman's hut before buying and some of the money made from the sale in France had had to go. But she was a cash buyer and there was no chain and the property was small and needed work so the price was lower than the average.

She quickens her step and fumbles in her pocket out of habit to check for the front door keys. And it is now that she hears it again. Someone breathing.

For the last week, she has stopped to look when she thought she heard breaths. But there was no one. Just a lurking shadow, a tumbling leaf somersaulting into the gutter. No one there but herself, whose breathing had quickened and whose heart beat uncomfortably in her chest. At night she would wake suddenly straining to hear sounds from the street outside. But hardly anyone was passing, for the road led nowhere.

Now as she presses herself against the alley wall, she knows for certain there is someone. She waits. A shout from afar is answered by a dog barking. Who is this person who follows? What are they seeking? Revenge? Money?

And then she hears the finite clue that tells her his identity. A very faint whistling as he breathes in and out. A flash of memory conjures up a picture of him sleeping; his breathing is regular, with a slight whistle on the out breath. An abiding happy memory of a time of content. Together sharing their lives and their habits.

The whistling stops as he speaks.

'Hallo.'

It is François. He is here, come to find her and take back what he gave so easily away.

'You stole my things.'

Her mouth is dry.

'You must have sold them all, I imagine.'

She nods. Dumb again. Inert with terror.

'I didn't say you could. I didn't say the silver.'

'You left a note. You said...'

Her voice is cracked, barely audible.

He comes into the alley and leans against the wall beside her. In the relatively short time apart, he is greatly changed. Older with greying hair and a glint in his dark eyes caught from the glare of the street lamp outside. There is stubble on his face.

He wants his silver back. He will have what is rightly his. He has fallen on hard times. He must have it back. She needs to recognise that. He means business.

His voice escalates with each short command. Her heart is rammed against her chest.

There is a smell of mould or damp about him which is suffocating.

'How...' She draws in a painful breath. 'How did you find me?'

'You found me,' he says, with an overarching pride. 'You're a fool. But then you know that.'

Her head is spinning. What is he saying?

'Found you? I don't understand.'

He grins, his teeth are broken and yellow.

'Where do you think I went?' he says, leaning back slightly, putting his head in the shadows. And she yelps in fear as his voice breathes into her ear.

'I came here. I came back to where I lived. Before I met you.' The last word spat out in scorn. 'You've followed me all the way home.'

She tries to contain her breathing, thoughts race ahead. She can't think about this now. It should have been Margate, not here. She should have gone further along. Further away. How could she have chosen the place where he was? How long had he been following? Which would be the best way to run?

His face is still invisible in the shadows.

The alley way is narrow; she can run only one way. He is heavier than before and she cannot squeeze past. Squeeze Gut Alley. Now she knows. She can run out and away from him but where? If she runs to the pub just up the street, will they help her? If she stays still, will he leave her alone? Or will he ignore her pleas for mercy? The answer comes as her arm is grabbed sharply and she is dragged down toward the beach. She is bundled like luggage over the sea wall. She stumbles onto the beach and he grabs her again, this time more roughly as she is hauled towards the water. Their feet slide and stumble making a crazy dance rhythm on the stones; both floundering across the surface to the sea. She tries to scream but he has a hand clamped over her mouth making it even harder to breathe. Her eyes cast about for help. But there is no-one. Car doors slam behind her in the car park. Surely someone will see her? Revellers beginning their Friday night. But the beach is dark now and the lights of the pubs and houses are dim and distant. The tide is retreating as if to say 'Sorry. You're on your own. Can't help you.'

As she falls to the unrelenting stones, she catches a glimpse of the skyline. The gash of light is just closing up for the night to come. She hopes it will be there tomorrow.

~~~

It was some hours before the body was found. One of the dog walkers saw her from the sea wall. The dog was all for exploring the inert shape but his master was uncertain. He reached for his phone.

At the hospital the new emergency was a mystery. She had no papers and no money on her and no phone. Her clothes were sodden. She was suffering from hypothermia and her pulse rate had plummeted. The police visited her bedside when she was awake but she was unable to give a description of the man. No, she didn't know him. Had never see him before. No she did not know why he had attacked her. No there was no-one she could call.

When they left, she shut her eyes tight, stemming the hot tears as best she could.

The nurses were kind and tried to get her to talk to them but she smiled politely and said that she was all right. Her recovery was slow and the fear relented in time and receded as the waves had done that night. If the tide had been in, she thought to herself, it would have been the end of me. And that was preferable to being here. He might be lying in wait for her all over again. She decided to reach for help.

The Detective who came to see her was attentive and professional throughout the interview. She told him all she knew but not all she feared. His name, his nationality, where they used to live, what he said and how he was dressed. The fear grew in her heart and she had to tell him that she was in fear of her life. He nodded and looked at her thoughtfully.

'Your description fits a man we arrested today,' he said. 'He's been taken into custody and is being interviewed.'

She looked away suddenly, trying to control the sobs of relief that rose in her throat.

The Detective got up and looked at her thoughtfully once more.

'I'll keep you posted,' he said and left.

~~~

The season has changed by the time she is able to go back to the sea. Now it is bright and triumphant; the diamonds in the distance rise and fall with the waves that dance smugly in the warm sunshine; a clean sky above them and a mirage on the skyline. And the tankers still lie in wait.

And the sounds of shrieking delights compete with the monstrous cry of gulls. And all around the voices of parents and their children tussle with each other for attention and young men shout to each other, hoping the girls with flowing hair will see them. But they pretend not to see them and gaze at the small screens snuggled in their well-manicured hands like trophies.

For the second time in her life she is putting the shattered pieces back together. She has been signed off from the hospital and is whole again in body and is working on her mind. She was offered counselling but declined it. Talking is still not an option but she is able to listen. She is offered advice by a professional, suited victim support worker and in the Crown Court her one-time lover is sentenced to a jail sentence in a high security prison in faraway London. She has time to escape once more.

She looks down at her feet and her new friend gazes up adoringly at her. She found him in the rescue centre and they fell in love at once. The new friend and she move up the beach to the dog walkers' circle and she waves at them as she passes. They are still talking, but not about her.

Oyster Wife

by Peggy Riley

Won't eat them now, when once they were my world.

Won't eat them now. Won't take that rough white shell into my rough red hands. Won't take the knife, won't twist the handle, won't prise them for their meat.

I'm wife to a dredgerman and his line goes back and back into time and tide. He said these waters had always held oysters, and his line always dredged them, smacks out scraping shingle and clay with the catch stick, raking and dragging the oyster bed clean. All for natives. It was hard work. Heavy work. Day in, day out, hauling the dredge in to see what he'd caught. Sole and squid, crabs and oysters, chipping the cultch with the cultick and shading the rest back out to sea. He'd load the catch in the baskets for oyster girls to sort and to grade and to pack for market. Hard, heavy baskets of shells for oyster girls like me.

Late, he'd come to my bed soaked with salt, damp limbed and dripping. Oftentimes, he'd turn out his pockets and show what he'd culled from the haul and kept back. Worthless things. Worthless to any but me. A pale pink cockle shell the size of his thumb. A bit of green glass worn smooth by the water. Once a tiny starfish, curled up in his hand like a stone, something he could keep safe in his holding.

When I married him, I wore lace on my head and my hair in waves. In my hand a bunch of mallow, lemon poppies, sea kale. I threw it to the air. I knew it was no use calling him in from the sea. Might as well bury him as call him up to land. He loved the sea, its moods and its changes. He loved never knowing what it would do.

What it had done.

Before, when I'd get mean at the sea, he'd tell me, 'Woman, you got to let things go through you like that oyster does.' And I'd say, 'An oyster starts out a man, ends up a woman, and then keeps changing back and forth.' Did he want that for me and all? He'd laugh at me then and I wouldn't mind it. I miss that laughing, now.

He loved his oysters, but I can't change. He loved his dredging, but I curse this sea. What it took from me. He's down there in it now, down in his seabed, and I can't catch him up. I'll hold my hard red heart clamped in so tight you'd have to kill me to open me. And what I'm working on – here, inside me – won't never turn to pearl.

Clouds like White Elephants

By Nick Hayes

They sat side by side but apart at the table. The children played on The Slopes and the man and woman looked out at the water and the horizon beyond. The heat of the day had passed and it was slipping into the early afternoon. They sipped at their coffee.

It's clear today. Really clear, said the man.

She stirred the coffee with her spoon.

I can see right across the water to the island. See the clouds hanging there. Like elephants.

He laughed at his joke. Clouds like white elephants.

She looked up from her stirring and peered into the distance. It wasn't a smile on her lips.

That's some clever joke, isn't it? Clever you. Clever you and stupid me for not getting it.

Come on, now. This was supposed to be a nice moment. Here at the Café. Overlooking the beach and the town. Our chance to take it all in.

She took in a rasping spiral of air. Yes, of course. Our chance to take it all in. But it's not the beach that is going anywhere, is it? Is it, Tom?

The man got up and stretched his arms towards the sea. He walked from the café tables to the long, concrete path leading down to the sea and bisecting the beach huts along the front. His eyes narrowed to see the children in the distance.

I told them to stay on The Slopes. They've gone right down to the bloody beach now. I'll go and get them. The tide's out but still. I think I'll go and get them. He looked to the woman for some affirmation which did not come.

He sat down. I'll leave them for now. We're nearly done here anyhow.

Nearly done, she echoed meaningfully. Yes, Tom, it would seem we are nearly done.

Come on, Charlie, you know we've been here before. We both know this is the only way forward. No reason to go through it all again. Not here. Not now. As he sat back in his seat his fingers reached for her grasp. She chose that moment to cradle her coffee in both hands and round her shoulders as she gazed into the distance.

The Street's catching the sun, she said. Out there, see. First thing we ever saw when we moved. Do you remember? We sat on that bench and ate chips while The Street came out of the sea like magic.

He swallowed and tugged at his chair to draw it closer. Course I remember, Charlie. Great days. Eh? We'll always have those, won't we? Just time to move on. Time to let the tide come in maybe? Think of it like that.

You arsehole, she cried. Don't ruin everything with your shit. This isn't some sort of game, you arse. This is our lives. All our lives. God, it's too much. It was her time to stand up and patrol the grass. Looking into the distance, carrying the mug in her hands and waving to the two children whose shapes bobbed some distance below on the shingle.

I'm going to call them up. Drink your coffee, Tom. It's time we started. Time to get off. Time for change, wasn't that how you put it? With those words she returned to the table and placed her mug loudly on the white of the table. She had approached him from behind, reaching across to return the coffee, and he took his chance. He grabbed hold of her arm, firmly but with tenderness.

It is time for a change. And we all know it's going to be tough.

But think of the money. Think of—

The bloody money! She shrieked and tore her body away. What kind of man are you, Tom? Open your eyes, can't you?

He froze for a moment. The other couple sitting outside at the café couldn't have failed to hear the emotion in that latest exchange. He felt the sting of embarrassment in his cheeks. He rummaged in his head for the right words. He'd been here before and he'd talked her round. This time it all seemed just a little too fraught. Just a little too emotional.

The woman angrily tidied up their belongings from the table, her head shaking a little and her body trembling. With his words having deserted him, Tom backed away from the scene and started to walk downwards to the beach and their children.

Two small figures ran from their adventures amongst the mud and shingle to greet their descending father. Their shoes long since discarded on the stones, their pink feet were streaked in mud and speckled with sand and grit, and their smiles were broad. Look, Dad, they choroused and held out hands full of treasure from the beach.

His language restored, he took each item from the children and gave a suitably enthusiastic word of amazement or appreciation. Who would have thought so many colours of stones? Not a tiny shell? Seaweed from the sea? Really! He conducted their explosion of joy and wonder with expert precision.

By now the family was complete, as his wife had crept down to meet them and they started to walk onto the beach to collect the abandoned shoes. The little boy ran ahead to scare some seagulls then yelp with pleasure. The little girl kept hold of her father's hand and whispered to him, almost inaudibly.

This is for you, she said and fished out something from the crescent pocket on the front of her pinafore dress.

Thank you, he chimed, barely looking at the object and adopting his approved tone for these beach events.

No look, Daddy, she insisted. Look. Look. It's my heart, she said.

In his hand she had placed a small, grey heart-shaped stone. The sea had worn its surface smooth and it gleamed at him. He stopped.

This is where my heart is, Daddy.

The woman stood beside them.

Is anyone listening in there, Tom?

He closed his palm around the smoothness of the pebble. You like it here, darling?

I love it! the little girl bellowed and ran after her brother.

He looked out to the white elephants and back to the pleading gaze of his wife. In his palm he thought he could feel the beat of the heart.

About Writers of Whitstable

by Joanne Bartley

Writing is hard, a bit like a marathon but inside your head. To get something finished takes endurance (not looking at Facebook), mental strength (writing even when you're not writing well) and hard work (turning bad lines into good ones.)

If you keep going, eventually you get to the finish line. But there no tape to break and no medal won, you just have words; a big pile of them, with no sense of whether anyone might want to read them. So you rearrange them all and wonder if they're any better. But you still don't know.

That's why I started Writers of Whitstable.

Part of me didn't want to know whether what I'd written was good or bad, but another part of me knew I had to find out. A few others felt the same and we met in the Horsebridge Centre to give it a try.

It wasn't a great start. Nobody took the lead and it was a shambles. At the next meeting only two people turned up, but they were nice people. At the next meeting somebody rewrote a new member's story. Another disaster.

But somehow we kept going. We moved to the Marine Hotel. We read each other's stories before meetings and tried to make sure feedback was honest but kind. One day I noticed I'd stopped being nervous about the meetings, and realised that lots of people, supportive and enthusiastic people, were creating new work every month. What's more, I'd written half a novel!

Then it got too successful. With so many people coming each month we split into two groups, one group for novels and one for short stories, and we now meet twice a month.

Then Lin, our editor and fantasy novel superstar, suggested we produce an anthology. At first I thought it was too ambitious, but here I am taking great pride in this finished book.

So here you'll find work from both experienced and novice writers, various styles, but all with the same enthusiasm both for writing and for Whitstable – all created by people who took an important step in finding an audience.

There are too many people to thank for helping to make Writers of Whitstable a success. Lin, our editor, is one of them, as well as all those who helped someone else get the best from their work. Also, our thanks to the Marine Hotel who put up with us and allow us to re arrange their furniture.

Lastly, if you have any interest in writing, check **writersofwhitstable.co.uk** for details of our group – we might just have room for another chair. One thing's for sure, we all understand that writing is hard, and scary, but also terrific fun, especially when you have a group of writer friends to share its ups and downs. I hope our enthusiasm comes through in the pages of this anthology.

Hermarnie Jesuiter

Hermarnie has travelled to hundreds of towns and dozens of countries as a travel writer and journalist. Her recent work as a writer for the Ruff Plannit Guides has seen her visit many of Britain's and Europe's places of interest and we are grateful to Hermarnie and her publishers for allowing us to include her 2015 review of Whitstable as the opening piece in this anthology.

In her successful career she has covered topics as varied as the fall of the Berlin Wall and the construction of the Thanet Way. When she finds the time between her hectic travel assignments, Hermarnie loves nothing better than curling up on the sofa with her two pet jaguars and a bottle of gin. Hermarnie is a keen Sucrologist and has one of the largest collections of sachets of sugar and brown sauce in the south of England.

Laura Sehjal

Laura is a self-employed drama teacher who owns her own company, Hatch Drama. Her main passion is life is teaching and helping the children who attend her classes to grow their confidence and creativity.

She has always written for the stage and has an MA in Theatre from the University of the Arts London, where she was baptised in the fires of creative hell, when she encountered her first crit. Since then she has managed to dust herself off and carry on putting her work out there.

Born and bred in Hull, East Yorkshire, Laura now finds herself living down south in Sturry. She has realised that the 'North / South divide' isn't as extreme as everyone had led her to believe and is having a whale of a time, even though no one knows what proper chip spice is down here!

When she isn't writing or working she also enjoys going on long walks with her incredibly bouncy dog, Bigsy, and making tatted jewellery.

John Wilkins

John writes because it gives him an extraordinary energy to believe in whatever comes next. It is a very contagious opportunity to set down some of his thoughts and imaginings. Writing in two genres, mystery and fantasy, offers him a map full of routes to plot his stories and develop characters both inside and outside the everyday existence.

He is currently working on two novels. After writing the first fifty thousand words of each in 2014 and 2015 respectively, with the help of Writers of Whitstable he is editing chapter by chapter. The first novel is about a woman who discovers the man who left her twenty-five years ago was an undercover police spy at the time. The other one is a fantasy novel about the quest of Martha to find the meaning of life, starting with her task of lifting the fog.

All of the above has been a journey of many footsteps since he persuaded Mick Jagger to lift his foot off the power cable at Earls Court back in the day...

Joanne Bartley

Jo has been writing since 1985 when a crush on Doyle in the Professionals led to her writing fan fiction instead of revising for her O levels. Notebook TV episodes somehow led to a degree in Scriptwriting for Film and TV. A highlight of her student days was a murder mystery script winning runner-up prize in a BBC competition; a lowlight was a producer asking 'whodunnit?' when she didn't have a clue.

Following university she found a few paid writing jobs, including a screenplay option for a film about a prize winning packet of crisps. The crisp movie was never made but she still believes snack movies may be the Next Big Thing.

Jo needed a better paid writing job so embarked on a career writing support emails for an online poker company. In 2008 Jo moved to Whitstable with her family and set up the Writers of Whitstable group. She's still pleased when she notices the words spell WoW.

Jo works in the gaming industry, chairs the Kent Education Network, runs the Museum of Fun community group, and operates **StoryPlanner.com**, a site offering plans for story structure. She occasionally finds time to write her novel.

James Dutch

James first attempted writing a story when he was just seven years old. He stapled several sheets of paper together and drew a picture of Yogi Bear and Boo Boo. Then he looked at the picture for a while, got writer's block and abandoned the project in time for tea, which was just as well as he probably would have been sued by Hannah Barbera for breach of copyright.

Jump forward thirteen years... Whilst working in the BBC research library, James started writing again. Most of it was not very good and ended up, quite rightly, in the recycling bin. This time however, he persevered, and another twenty years on, he is still writing. He is currently working on the second draft of his second novel (the first, unpublished, is still languishing in the bottom of a drawer somewhere...) and no longer gets writer's block, only ever settling down to write a story that he's allowed to grow in his mind until it's just begging to be written down.

James lives in Canterbury with his wonderful partner, who is always his first and most trusted reader, and their 5 year old son, who has just written his first book which consisted of twelve words and is called The Hungry Monster. He is a proud Dad!

Kim Miller

Kim is a new writer, joining the Whitstable group in 2015 to finally start writing after decades of prevaricating. So far she has concentrated on short stories, still trying to find her style and areas of interest. Naturally, she has an idea for a novel brewing in the background and will, hopefully, have the courage to start it soon(ish). She enjoys many kinds of books, classic and contemporary, and is in love with EF Benson's Mapp and Lucia.

Kim lives in the nearby coastal village of Oare and can see Whitstable from the home she shares with her partner, Andrew; their daughter, Daisy, is at university studying politics.

Nick Hayes

Nick has been teaching in local secondary schools for nearly 20 years but still has plenty to learn. He has been writing since he was able to hold a pen and his handwriting remains largely unchanged since his first effort – 'Sugar in Space' (aged five and three-quarters).

When he emerges from beneath his marking he enjoys writing poetry and short stories but doesn't think he has the stamina just yet for a novel, although he harbours dreams of being the next teacher-turned-author like David Almond and Phillip Pullman.

In an alternative universe he wrote The Great Gatsby, the poems of Edward Thomas and all the strips from Peanuts. In this world he largely spends time with his family and two recently acquired cats. Any excess energy he spends on tending his long term illness – an obsession for Aston Villa.

Writers of Whitstable have been instrumental in encouraging him from thinking about doing more writing to actually doing more writing. He has come to agree with John Cheever – 'I can't write without a reader. It's precisely like a kiss—you can't do it alone.'

RJ Dearden

RJ Dearden is the author of 'The Realignment Case', a sci-fi thriller about time manipulation. RJ and his wife moved to Whitstable in 2000 and have lived happily here since. They have a young son and survive on four hours' sleep a night.

For his day job, RJ works in London as an IT infrastructure manager. His current WIPs are a sci-fi dystopian mystery set in 2065 and a Anglo-French screen comedy about sport. He urges you to buy 'The Realignment Case' novel in large volumes and persuade Hollywood to buy the rights for the film.

AJ Ivory

Amanda stumbled on Whitstable many years ago as a student and decided this was the only place in the UK she would want to stay. She has lived in France, Africa and the Middle East.

She studied in Kent, sometimes escaping from the campus, catching the bus to Whitstable, and hiding away with the books upstairs in Tea and Times.

She has always loved writing but has never done anything serious with it. The writing group is a great way to build up confidence and test ideas on an unsuspecting audience.

In real life she has taught English, worked as a tour guide, an au pair, waitressed in lousy restaurants in Cape Town, had a remarkably unsuccessful part-time career selling roses to romantic couples when a student, and latterly has carved out a career in the legal profession.

She is currently working on a series of short stories and possibly a novel.

Alison Kenward

Alison started life in Exeter; the highpoint of the week as a teenager was a Church barn dance every Sunday evening so she joined a drama group and began acting. She soon became a leading light in the drama group and auditioned successfully for Drama School and spent three blissful years doing what she liked best. Now a star-struck actress, she fully expected to become famous. This delusion continued for a while until she got a proper job teaching.

Some years later, she returned to the 'biz' only to find that parts for women of a certain age consisted of putting on a maid's outfit and serving lamb chops. So she began writing her own leading roles for the stage. She's now on her fourth play and, along the way, has been lured into short story competitions which promise cash prizes. As yet, none have come her way but it has developed her writing ability. One story, 'Susan's Number', has been e-published and waits in a darkened corner of the internet for publishers to note. She has also written a long story but hesitates to call it a novel. Okay, it is a novel but it remains on the hard drive and in many different drafts. However, nothing daunted, she continues to write for stage and screen in between producing, directing and acting and is practising her Bafta prize winning speech for most promising newcomer.

Alison lives in Whitstable and is Artistic Director of Kent Coast Theatre.

Lin White

Lin is an avid reader, and has been making up stories in her head for as long as she can remember. The Internet brought the realisation that others enjoy that sort of thing as well, and she soon discovered fanfiction.

Writing original fiction was the logical next step. To date there are three novels in various levels of completion, plus a bunch of short stories.

In her real life, she has been involved in publishing and education for many years and currently works as an editor and proofreader, helping other writers to polish up their work ready for publication.

She also runs regularly, and enjoys life with her husband, three sons, three cats and a dog.

Phillip Mind

Phillip has lived in Whitstable for eighteen years. He was brought up in the Medway Towns and attended university in London and Loughborough. He works in London and occasionally writes short stories and poems, starting more than is ever finished. His story for the anthology will be his first to make it to print and part of a wider project to build a portfolio of finished work.

Phillip's first job was in the London Library, the largest private library in the country, where he started to read and love literature and he hasn't stopped reading voraciously since. His favourite writer is Milan Kundera – like the celebrated Czech writer, he is interested in how small gestures shape the larger events of life.

He is currently working on a play about a group of men who take a daytrip on a red London bus and return twelve hours later re-shaped by their experience.

David Williamson

David specialises in short story fiction and has been a regular contributor to Writers of Whitstable since it was first established. David's observational style of writing exploits the pleasures and dilemmas of modern life and roots them in universal themes of love, loss and regret, often with bizarre twists and poignant conclusions.

In his spare time David runs the social enterprise **andmakeitbetter.net** and regularly exhibits his artwork at regional galleries. Both David's art and writing are inspired by the villages and countryside of Kent, his home county of Yorkshire and the West Coast of Ireland. David's new collection of stories *The Lovers of Today* is soon be published.

Trust Sulha – our charity

Writers of Whitstable are proud to support Trust Sulha, which in its turn supports the education of young Afghan refugees who live in Pakistan. Since 2006, these young people have been supported by a committed group of volunteers from Whitstable. The connection was made when one of the volunteers went to Pakistan and met an Afghan refugee woman called Jamilla Abassy.

Jamilla and her husband Nabi were not teachers when they fled Afghanistan in 1992 but soon after they arrived, Jamilla was so upset at seeing Afghan children rummage through rubbish for things to sell, that she decided to open a school. Overwhelmed by demand, Jamilla taught in stairwells and on rooftops. Students who could not afford to pay were taught for free.

Jamilla defied the Taliban with co-educational classrooms and said she hoped there would be a new battle in Afghanistan – the battle of the pen. Her words were recently echoed by the Nobel Prize winning girls' education activist Malala Yousafzai: 'Our books and our pens are our most powerful weapons.'

Jamilla and her colleagues now teach 2,000 students who follow the Afghan National Curriculum. Wonderfully, in the last year more than 60 young people have graduated from these refugee schools and are attending universities in Pakistan and Afghanistan to study subjects from engineering to midwifery.

It costs just £24 to educate a student this way. Please contact this book's producers if you would like more information or to help.